EFF THIS DIET

KRISSY V

To all of the diet warriors. You are beautiful!
Once you believe it, you will see your beauty!

Be yourself and be happy!

CONTENTS

LETTER TO MY READERS!

As always this is hard! I wrote this book originally for an anthology – Life After Losing.

I was listening to Mika's song, *You Are Beautiful*, and the subject of this book came into my mind. It is a very personal subject to me as I have struggled with my weight in the last five years.

I take medication which made me put on weight originally, now my eating habits aren't great and I still take the medication so it seems the chances of being a 'skinny minny' again are *slim!*

I shed many tears during the writing this book, not because it's sad – because it's not. But because I felt like I was in therapy and wanted to stand up and say, "My name is Krissy V and I am fat!"

So, I think firstly I need to thank myself for being so

honest and putting pen to paper to write about something that means a lot to me. I don't want anyone to think I am fat shaming – because I'm not.

I am Kayleigh in this story.

She is me!

As always, I want to say thank you to Natasha for always being there for me:- morning, noon and night whenever I need to talk.

Jen, you rock. You have been my rock and I hope I've been yours.

Karen Sanders, thank you for being my editor and understanding my rubbish that appears on the page. You always make it better!

Karen Frances, you know how I feel about you so thank you as well for listening to me when I didn't think I was writing about the right thing and for telling me to do it.

Lastly, and by no means least – thank you to my

readers. I hope I've done you proud and you enjoy my story.

Most people can relate to Kayleigh and her weight struggles and I hope you understand her like I do!

Thank you all

Krissy V

PROLOGUE

Big girl you are beautiful

It feels like Mika is singing about me when I hear his song, except I'm not beautiful ... I'm just fat!

When someone asks you to describe yourself, I bet you say, 'blonde, brunette, tall, short.' I just say fat.

You can picture me now: blonde, medium height, and fat. I didn't want to be fat, no one ever does, but I am, and I have to either live with it or do something about it.

Believe me, I have tried to do something about it. I think I've spent enough money at 'Fat Club' over the last few years that I could have paid for liposuction AND a couple of tummy tucks.

So, enough about me. This is my story, and I hope you enjoy it.

1
FAT CLUB

"DARRAGH, I'm off to Fat Club. I'll see you later," I shout, as I head out the door. I don't hear his reply.

Darragh is one of my roommates. He's six foot two inches, gorgeous, and I love him. We're really close. Do I have feelings for him? Am I attracted to him? Hell yeah! I have a pulse, of course I'm attracted to him. I think even a nun would be attracted to him.

Do you know what makes him more attractive? He's a really nice guy. Like, seriously 'nice'. He would help anyone, he would do anything for me and looks after me so much. We've been friends for years. I never thought our friendship would last, but it has. He's a model who goes to the gym every day for hours on end. He looks after himself, and his body is so well sculpted … yes, I've drooled about his body after 'accidentally' walking into the bathroom when he'd just got out of the shower. It's no coincidence that the door doesn't lock anymore. I really don't know how the lock got bent like that. I laugh to myself. Fifteen minutes of hard work that's how…

I get into my car, drive for ten minutes, and then get out at the local school hall. I know I should walk, but that's too much like hard work. Fat Club is held every Monday evening. I try to go every week, but sometimes I just can't be arsed to be embarrassed anymore and then I'll give up. I pay ten euro for someone to tell me that I've put on weight, I've maintained my weight, or in rare circumstances, I've lost some weight.

Do you know how humiliating it can be?

No. Because you don't need to go to Fat Club. Let me tell you that, some weeks, I walk out of that school hall and I'm about two inches shorter than when I walked in.

Monday night is treat night. So, regardless of what the scales say, I always have a treat on a Monday night. Usually a Curly Wurly which has been in the freezer (making it last longer because it's harder to chew) or a cake, or something high in calories and *really* bad for me. Darragh usually buys me something, and we sit down together and eat in silence.

I've paid my money and I step up on the scales. "So, how do you think you did this week?" the girl behind the scales asks.

I know it's rude, but I don't know her name. I don't really want to know the name of the person who tells me week after week that I'm putting on weight and paying for the privilege.

"The week was good, but it's the weekends that I find hard. If only I could be weighed on a Thursday or a Friday then I'm sure it would be better," I moan, as I stand on the scales.

"Well done, Kayleigh. You've lost four pounds this week. Whatever you've done … keep it up."

"Seriously? Let me get off and stand on them again. That can't be right." I step off the dreaded scales.

She laughs as she takes my card out and puts it back in again. "Yeah, you've definitely lost four pounds. Well done!"

She writes down my loss and hands back my book and card. I step off and put on my socks, shoes, jewellery, glasses, and anything else I had taken off before I weighed myself.

———

I walk around the room and then take a seat; I'm in a daze. It's amazing how much more motivated I feel than usual.

I stay for the meeting, and our leader, Sophie, reads out who has lost weight and who might be unhappy as they put on weight. Thank God I'm not one of those people tonight.

"Kayleigh, well done. Four pounds lost and never to be seen again!"

I snicker to myself. Yeah, right. If only!

"What did you do differently this week?" she asks me.

I think long and hard about it and can't think what I did differently, except I got absolutely trollied on Saturday night and spent all Sunday puking my guts up. No, I don't think I will tell her that. Maybe that's what I need to do every week. I'll ask Darragh what he thinks about that.

"Nothing, really. I think I prepared my meals a bit better than normal." Well, that was true. I had prepared well last week.

"Good. Preparation is key. You need to rinse and repeat last week and then hopefully you will lose more next week too. Well done, Kayleigh."

I nod my head and drift off as she goes through the rest of the Fat Clubbers.

I think about Darragh. I secretly love him. I daydream about being with him, and in that daydream, I'm super skinny. He likes super skinny girls. You should see the girls that come out of his bedroom on a Sunday lunchtime. Wow! They are smoking hot!

Yes, I'm jealous. I know we're friends, but come on, when you see someone that gorgeous in barely any clothes, you're going to think about how he is under the engine, if you know what I mean. He gets my engine started all the time.

I realise the meeting is finished and everyone is making their way out of the school hall. I jump in the car and text Darragh to let him know how I got on.

Kayleigh: I lost four pounds this week. Can't believe it.
Darragh: Well done babe, you worked hard this week.

I don't dare tell him I cheated. Let him think I did well.

Kayleigh: Thanks. Hope you have a nice treat for me.

Darragh: You'll have to wait and see. See you in a few minutes

Kayleigh: KK

––––––

I drive the ten minutes home and part of my Fat Club ritual is to play Mika's '*Big Girl you are Beautiful*' song, it is kind of like my anthem. By the time I get home I'm really excited as I walk through the door.

I find Darragh waiting for me in the kitchen; he's leaning against the countertop in low-slung sweat pants and a tight fitting t-shirt. God, he makes me drool.

As soon as I walk in, he hugs me and swings me around. "Well done, Kay. I'm so proud of you. You're going to do it this time. I just know."

"Thanks, but I think it was a fluke."

"No way. I know you prepared your meals in advance, so do it again this week and see what happens."

"Did you get me something nice?" I ask, trying to move him from the countertop.

He laughs and stands there so I can't budge him. Eventually he moves out of the way and I see a large coconut macaroon. One of my favourites!

I reach up and kiss him on the cheek. "Thanks," I say, blushing. He makes me feel so self-conscious, and I wish I could tell him how I feel, but I don't want to lose him as a friend. Maybe, when I'm slimmer, he will like me differently.

———

It's that thought that motivates me this time.

We sit in the lounge on the sofa, watching TV and eating our macaroons. I know he shouldn't be eating them with his fitness regime, but he does it for me. I lean into his side and his arm goes around my shoulder while we watch a film.

Embarrassingly, I fall asleep, and only wake up when he puts me down on my bed. "Oh my God. Darragh, did you carry me upstairs?"

"Of course I did. It's not the first time, you know?" he says, smiling.

"Oh my God. I'm so embarrassed. You should have woken me up. You'll break your back carrying me up those stairs." I blush. I hate him knowing how heavy I am.

"Don't be so stupid. Have you seen my muscles?" He flexes his biceps.

I laugh; he's so silly.

"See you in the morning, Kay," he says, blowing me a kiss as he walks out of my room.

I lay there for a while before I snuggle under the covers to go to sleep. I'm proud of myself tonight.

I need to keep this up. I want Darragh, and I'm going to get him. I just hope he's interested in me when I'm skinnier; it's the one thing that keeps me going.

2
PREPARATION IS KEY

It's only been two days since Fat Club and I'm bored of 'preparing' my meals already. I really want to have a Chinese takeaway, but I force myself to keep going. Darragh is my ultimate goal. I need to really try this time.

My other roommate, Shane, walks into the kitchen as I'm about to stick my finger in the chocolate spread jar. I pull it back just in time. Or so I think.

"God, Kayleigh, were you just about to take a finger full of chocolate spread?" He looks at me in disgust.

We have a love/hate relationship. He loves to hate me. I don't know why he doesn't like me, but I usually stay out of his way.

"What if I was?" I say, with my hands on my hips.

"I thought you were dieting AGAIN," he says, staring at me. When he looks me up and down, it makes my skin crawl. He is gorgeous too. I don't know how I ended up with two gorgeous roommates, but that is the hand I was dealt.

"I AM dieting, thank you!" I scream at him. God, he infuriates me so much. "Not that it's got anything to do with you!" I storm up to my room.

I throw myself down on the bed. Why does he annoy me so much? It's like he doesn't like me because I'm fat. How stupid is that?

I sulk for about five minutes in my room and then I go back downstairs to prepare tomorrow's meals. It takes a lot of hard work, this dieting lark. I wish I could just wake up and be two or three stone lighter. That would be great.

I've tried it all.

Diet pills – they made me spend hours on the toilet and then run around with so much energy, like I was on speed or something. My heart started palpitating badly and I thought I was going to have a heart attack. So, after the third attempt, I finally realised that diet pills are not a good choice for me.

Atkins diet – eating all protein and no carbs. That's really hard to do. No bread or pasta. Like, what else is there to eat if you take those out of your diet? And the bad breath it gives you is horrendous. People can smell you coming a mile off. Great results in a short period of time, but it left me with headaches, heart palpitations, and high cholesterol.

Intragastric balloon – yeah, I tried it. I wouldn't advise it to anyone. It's relatively simple to do. Day surgery, in and out in a couple of hours. The balloon is inflated slowly, and once it is fully inflated, it means less room in your stomach, so therefore you feel fuller sooner and stop eating as much. Sounds great, right? Yeah, I lost weight alright, but that's because I had to go on a liquid diet for a while; nothing but liquefied food. I felt like a baby all over again. Unfortunately for me, the balloon kept inflating and I was in a lot of pain so I had to have it taken out. Once I got over that, I couldn't fill my stomach with enough food, and guess what? I put on more weight!

Cabbage Soup diet – do I need to explain this one? I think everyone has tried this at some stage in their life, however big or small they might be. The taste? The smell? The after effects? Yeah. Not worth doing this one either. It's no wonder I'm single after that diet.

Fat Club – this is the one that seems to work for me, but I relapse and then put the weight back on again. I need to be motivated and stick to it then it will work well. Sure, Susie down the road lost three stone in ten months on the Fat Club diet. I wish I had her determination.

Anyway, I digress with all the failed attempts I've had at dieting. Shane only moved in with us about four months ago. He's about six foot tall, stocky build, and he takes care of himself too. He is another one with a revolving bedroom door at the weekend.

My bedroom door is squeaky and rusty as it doesn't open often enough – if you know what I mean.

I can't remember the last time I brought a guy back to my room.

Let me think for a minute.

Yeah, I think it was Tom. Or was it Steve? No, it was Aaron, and he was so drunk he couldn't get it up. So, it has been a VERY long time since my lady garden saw some action. You all know about Charlotte's web, well I've got Kayleigh's web! I think it has been that long since I had sex that I'm a born again virgin and my hymen has grown over.

People just don't want to shag a fat person. It doesn't matter how pretty you are, how nice you are, how well you get on with someone. They don't want to see what is under those control pants and vest! I don't know why; it's like a treasure trove under my Spanx.

I don't think Shane can see past my fat to see the real me. Darragh knows the real me and I don't think he takes any notice of my size, but someone like him wouldn't look twice at someone like me.

There's a knock at the door, and when it opens, Maeve, my best friend, walks in. "Hey there," she says, leaning against the door jamb to the kitchen. "What are you doing?"

"I'm preparing," I say, as I chop my cucumber for my 'gorgeous' salad.

She laughs. "How long is that going to last this time?"

"I'm going to do it this time. I have to. I hate the way people like Shane look at me. They can't see past my excess flab to see the real me and that pisses me off."

"They're not worth it, babe. Look at Darragh. He sees the real you. He's never put off by your size," she says, helping herself to a lager from the fridge.

"Yeah, but he would never shag me though, would he?" I say huffily, as I put my dressing in a separate container.

"Who says I wouldn't?" I hear Darragh say, chuckling as he comes into the kitchen.

Maeve spits her drink out as she laughs. "Ooh, God!"

I blush. "D ... Darragh, erm, we were just ... erm."

He laughs. "Don't worry about it, Kay, but don't put yourself down." He puts his arms around me and pulls me in for a hug. "I'd so give you one," he whispers in my ear.

I push him away. "Darragh!"

"What? I'm only telling the truth. You don't realise how gorgeous you are. You can't see past your weight, but there's more to you than what's on the outside." He smiles at me.

"Th ... thanks," I stutter. I turn back around and start moving things around the place when they don't really need to be moved.

How embarrassing!

Maeve is giggling to herself, and Darragh has helped himself to a beer as well. He hands me a lager too. I should say no, but ... I need a drink after that comment.

I finish making meals for the next day then we go into the lounge to relax for a bit.

One beer turns into five beers, and my counting

'fat points' goes out the window. Then the pizza comes. I don't know who ordered that! Oops.

Maeve and I decide it will be really funny to make Darragh watch *Fifty Shades of Grey*. It will be fun to watch him squirm!

Except it doesn't turn out that way. He doesn't squirm … I do!

I end up sitting next to him, obviously. I always do. And I keep trying to sneak glances to see if he is 'enjoying' the film. I can't help myself! Men look at women's tits, I look at men's packages. Shoot me!

Watching Jamie Dornan work his charm on Dakota Johnson (who, by the way, is stick thin!) makes me horny.

When he spanks her, I clench my arse cheeks.

Just the thought of being in bed with Jamie Dornan really gives me twinges in my vajajay! Then, as I drink more, Jamie is starting to look like Darragh. Yep, this is about to get uncomfortable.

We drink more. At some stage, Maeve left, but I don't remember when or why as the movie is still on. Darragh has his arm around me and his thumb is rubbing circles on my shoulder.

He keeps kissing my head.

I keep moving closer. Not that I can get much closer. But I really want to.

"You know you're beautiful, Kay, don't you?" he says into my head. Well, that's what I think he says. He could be telling me to lay off the lager, but I'm sure that's what he says.

"Hmm," I say, rather than being committal.

"You're perfect, do you know that?"

He is seriously pissed.

"Darragh, I can't carry you to bed, you know? So, don't get too drunk. I'd have to leave you on the couch, babe."

"You don't need to carry me, babe. I'll carry you any day." He slides down the couch a bit, bringing me with him.

"Darragh, we need to go to bed. We can't stay here all night."

"Now, that's the best offer I've had all night." He laughs.

"Darragh!" I say, punching his arm.

He tips my chin up so I'm looking at him. "No, seriously, Kay. I've waited a long time to hear you say that to me."

He leans down and his lips are extremely close to mine. Is he going to kiss me? I know I've dreamt of this, BUT do I really want him to kiss me? Will it change our relationship? Do I really give a shit about that? Yes, I want him to kiss me. I dream about it every night.

I lean closer to him. Then I realise that we're friends who are drunk and nothing more. We will never be anything more than drunk friends having a fumble. He doesn't want a relationship with me. He wants someone like super skinny Susie down the road.

I move my head at the last minute and he kisses my forehead instead.

"Kay, you moved!" he says, shaking his head. "Don't you want to kiss me?"

He looks hurt. His eyes are looking down and his bottom lip is pouting.

"Of course I do, but we're friends. Friends first. I'm not your type at all. You're just drunk."

I try to get off the couch and he grabs my arm and pulls me back down, and before I know it, he's on top of me, kissing me.

No, sorry. He's not kissing me, he is eating my face. What's going on? I don't care. I eat his face back.

"I want you so bad, Kay."

I must be really drunk because I think he just said he wants me.

"Darragh, I have to go to bed. I think I'm drunk."

He chuckles. "Always have an excuse, don't you?"

What is he talking about?

He gives me one last kiss and then gets off the sofa.

He holds out his hand. "Come on. It's time for bed."

My eyebrows rise.

"Don't worry - separately!" he says, as I take his hand and he pulls me out of the room.

I climb into bed and wonder what the hell went on tonight.

3
HALF A STONE AWARD

"Oh my God, I'm so hungover!" Darragh says, dragging himself into the kitchen. "What the hell happened last night? I thought we were having a quiet Wednesday night in."

I laugh to myself. There are advantages of having a little extra weight; I don't get hungover as much as anyone else.

"We wiped out the beer fridge last night."

Yes, we have a beer fridge, which is separate to our food fridge.

"No wonder I feel like shit!" He takes the black coffee I just made for him.

At least he won't remember our kisses. Maybe it's his way of saving me from being embarrassed.

"Right, well, I'm off to work. I'll see you later." I walk out of the kitchen, and when I get to the front door, I hear him shout.

"Kayleigh, wait!"

My heart is racing. Is he going to try and kiss me? Surely not!

"Here," he says. "You don't want to spoil all your hard work."

I look down to see what he's giving me. My prepared food for the day. I groan and take it off him.

When I look up at him, he's smiling at me. "Thanks, Darragh. I'll see you later."

All day at work, I just want to go to the shop next door and buy some chocolate, but I resist. I think about Darragh a lot today. Maybe if I can lose the weight then he might want to make a go of a relationship or something. My weight must be holding him back or he would have said something this morning.

After work, I cook myself some chicken, sweet potato wedges, and a salad. It was actually really tasty. All I need to do is make that small bit of effort and I'll lose some more weight.

I don't see either of my roommates until Sunday night, although I met the steady line of women leaving their rooms, sometimes more than one at a time. Blimey! But they were all the same: skinny, petite, and beautiful. Everything I'm not! Sometimes it feels like I'm having my face rubbed in it. I hear the girls giggling and then see them coming down the stairs in their really short, barely there dresses. I wouldn't even get one leg in some of those dresses let along a whole body. Do I ever think about how I would look in one of those bondage dresses, oops sorry bandage dresses? Yes of course I do, but all I can picture is the lumps and bumps that will be sticking out, I would look like the *Michelin* man if I had a white dress on.

Monday rolls around and it's off to Fat Club again. I drive to the school hall and stand in line to be humiliated.

"Hi, Kayleigh. How do you think you did this week?" the girl asks me.

"I had a blowout during the week, but otherwise I've been quite good. I'd expect to lose at least a pound tonight."

I stand on the scales and watch the numbers going up and up and up. They're getting closer to last week's weight. Then they move up and down a fraction, and then they stop. I look at the number and then back at her.

"Well done, Kayleigh. You've lost six pounds this week. Whatever you've been doing is paying off. Keep it up. You've got your half stone award tonight."

"No way, really?" I've never had an award before! I usually go up and down in weight but never actually get anywhere.

"Yes. Well done. I hope you're staying for the class so you can collect your first piece of bling!" She is so excited, and I can feel it rubbing off on me.

"I will be. Thanks!"

When I sit down, I can't sit still. This is something new for me. Bling on the front of your Fat Club book is something to be proud of. I text Maeve and Darragh.

Maeve: OMG that is amazing. Well done, you need to get pissed during the week more often if that's the case.

Kayleigh: I know LOL

It takes Darragh longer to text back, and when my phone vibrates, it's at the same time that my name is called.

"Ten pounds lost, never to be seen again. Well done, Kayleigh, with a loss of six pounds tonight."

Everyone claps and I blush.

"So, what did you do differently this week?"

"I prepared everything and was just extra careful what I did and didn't eat. I think the weight loss the week before made a big difference to me."

"Yes, it can motivate you to lose more, for sure."

She moves onto the next person and I take out my phone; it's Darragh.

Darragh: Well done Kay, I am so proud of you.

Kayleigh: Thanks

Darragh: So do you still want a treat tonight? I have something I know you are going to love.

Kayleigh: What is it? Tell me

Darragh: No, decide if you want it or not.

Kayleigh: Darragh of course I want a treat, this is me you're talking to.

Darragh: OK, then it will be waiting for you when you get home.

I wonder what it is. I'm feeling antsy now, but

thankfully, I don't have long to wait until the class is over.

"Before you go, next week is taster night. So bring along something you like making for yourself and share it with everyone else."

I wonder what I can make and bring in. I don't think she will appreciate me bringing in some cans of lager!

I jump in my car and drive home, excited about what Darragh might have bought for me as a treat.

Pushing the door open, I shout, "Hi, honey! I'm home!"

When I go into the kitchen, Darragh is sitting at the table, waiting for me. He has the biggest smile on his face, and sitting in front of him on a plate is my favourite cake in the world. There's only one bakery that does it in our area and it's not easy to get to.

"Oh my God! You got me an egg custard! How? When?" I run over to him and kiss him on the cheek. "Thank you so much."

I lean forward and sniff it. I have a habit of sniffing my food. I don't know why, but I've done it for years.

He laughs. "You're welcome, Kay. I know you love them so I went and got it for you today."

We sit and eat them; of course, he bought himself one too. He never liked them, but he's got used to them over the last year or so.

"You've done really well, Kay. Are you interested in starting at the gym yet?" he asks, taking a bite of his custard.

I nearly spit mine out. "Darragh, you know I don't exercise." I laugh. "Can you imagine me in gym clothes? I won't look like those ladies you work out with every day, you know?"

He smiles at me. "You're always putting yourself down. You need to stop doing that. You are so much sexier than the girls in the gym. You have curves in all the right places. They have no shape and granny arses."

"Granny arses? What are they?" I say, laughing at him.

"Granny arses are flat bums. Well, they don't have bums at all, they're just flat up and down. Guys don't find that attractive. I don't think it matters what guys say, they all want something to grab hold of."

He shocks me. I always think guys want skinny girls; that's why no one wants me, or why I think no one wants me.

"Really? You're just saying that to make me feel better." I nudge him.

"No, seriously, Kay. If you sleep with someone who is skin and bone, you think you're going to break their bones and you have to be gentle. With curvy girls, you can grab hold and go as hard as you like."

I blush. The thought of him grabbing hold and going hard has my temperature rising.

He laughs, and I don't know if he's serious or not.

"Kay, if you want to start working out at the gym, let me know, and I can be your personal trainer. There are some exercises that won't suit you, so we can work on the right stuff."

"I'll never be serious about the gym, you know that, right?"

"I know, and to be honest, I don't want you to get obsessed with it, just use it for toning up. You seem to have got this losing weight lark down to a tee, so that would be the next step."

"Are you telling me I'm fat?" I ask, pretending to be annoyed.

"No way. You know I don't see you like that." He takes my hands. "Surely you know that by now."

"I'm only joking with you, Darragh. Relax! I have to say that I feel a lot more confident now I've lost over half a stone. I can't really feel the difference. Well, maybe a little bit, but I want to know what it feels like to be a stone lighter. I don't want to lose stones and stones, just enough to not feel fat!"

"Why do you keep saying you're fat? You're not at all." He pulls me down on his lap. "Look at me!" he says, using his finger to move my chin so I'm looking at him. "Kayleigh, you are beautiful, you just need to believe in yourself and become more confident in yourself. Only then will you believe how beautiful you are." He looks like he's staring into my soul. He knows what scares me the most.

"Thanks, Darragh. I know, but in my mind, being skinny means being confident."

He shakes his head and leans his forehead against mine. "One day ... one day you'll see it yourself." He kisses me very gently on the lips and then pulls away.

I stand up awkwardly, and just as I'm about to ask him about his kiss, Shane walks in.

He looks at the table. "What's the celebration?"

"Kayleigh got her half stone award!" Darragh says with pride.

"Really?" Shane says, looking at me. It feels like

he's undressing me with his eyes. I feel violated. He just doesn't look at me the same way Darragh does. He doesn't see me the way Darragh does.

I stand up from Darragh's lap. "Yeah, can't you tell?" I ask, giving him a twirl.

"Erm, so erm, you're really going for the diet this time, are you? Can't wait to see how long this one lasts. Right, I'm off to work. See you guys later." Shane walks out.

"God, he's so miserable unless he's shagging some blonde bimbo or two," I say, gathering my lunch and snacks together.

"So, you avoided the question. Are you going to let me take you to the gym? We can just do toning exercises. We don't have to do any cardio unless you really want to," Darragh says, leaning back against the worktop with his arms folded.

"Urgh, okay then. I'll give it a go. But nothing too strenuous to start with. I haven't done any exercise in a couple of years." I look at him and see his raised eyebrows. "Don't judge me!" I turn back to preparing my food.

"Great. The hardest part is saying yes. We can start tomorrow night. Get yourself some gym gear and I'll meet you at my gym at about seven. Is that okay?"

"I suppose so. God, you're annoying. Get out of my sight."

He laughs and leaves the kitchen to go to bed.

When I think about him with all those skinny, beautiful gym bunnies, it makes me feel sick. He is going to be so embarrassed to be seen with me tomorrow night.

4
GYM BUNNY OR GYM ELEPHANT?

The next day, I head to the sports shop, in my lunchtime, to buy myself some leggings and a top. Looking around, there aren't many larger sizes. Do larger girls not work out? It makes me mad. Just because I'm big, doesn't mean I don't want to do what my skinny counterparts want to do.

I decide to head over to one of the chain stores and look at their selection. They actually have a lot of choice, and I end up getting a pair of black leggings with a pink stripe down the side. Then I match it with a bright pink singlet with a racer back, and a black see through t-shirt with 'Muscles or Mascara' on it in pink. Next, I look at the runners and pick a black pair that will go with everything. Finally, I need to buy a sports bra to hold these puppies in, because if I don't, I'm going to end up with two black eyes.

Darragh better appreciate the effort I'm putting in here!

When I get back to my desk, my cellmate – well, we do work in cubicles in here – Natalie, asks what I bought. When I show her, she starts laughing.

"You need to send me a picture of you wearing that, hun. I can't quite see it somehow."

"Don't be so mean. I know I don't look like the picture of health, and I know I look like I don't work out; that's because I don't. But I am determined to do this. I really am."

"Sorry, Kayleigh, but it's just not something I associate you with."

"Me neither, Natalie, but I need to do something. Darragh says I don't need to do cardio and just to do some toning exercises at first."

"Ah, so that's why you're going to do this! Darragh! Mind you, I would do whatever that fine thing asks me to do too."

"Shut up. We know you like Darragh, you throw yourself at him often enough," I say, laughing. Darragh has no interest in Natalie, even though she could be one of his gym bunnies.

"Yeah, not that it does me any good. He's never interested."

I turn away from her and go back to my computer.

The afternoon flies by, and it's not long before

I'm in the bathroom, changing into my gym gear. You can laugh; it makes me laugh too when I talk about gym gear. After I've managed to pull the tight leggings on and make sure I've not got a camel toe - you know that happens when you have them too tight, right? Well, after sorting that little problem out, I take a look at myself in the full-length mirror. Turning around, I think I don't look too bad, but when I see the size of my arse, I panic. Oh my God, what if he makes me bend over in front of him? It will be like a lunar eclipse.

I shake my head and gather my things. Putting my coat on, I walk out to my car. Driving over to the gym, my nerves kick in. Maybe I should just drive right past and go home and hide.

No. Darragh would kill me if I don't turn up now after agreeing to it.

Pulling up outside the gym, I take a deep breath and then collect my new bag with a towel and a bottle of water in it. I text Darragh.

Kayleigh: Hey hun, I'm just coming in. Will you meet me in reception? I'm really nervous and might just turn around and go home for a big, fat, juicy cream cake

It doesn't take him long to answer.

Darragh: You have no stamina Kay, I'll be there in two mins

Kayleigh: Thanks hun

I open the glass door, and as soon as I step through, I can smell chlorine, sweat, and aftershave. What a mixture.

"Hi, can I help you?" a pretty, petite, sexy blonde bimbette says from the reception desk.

"Erm, I'm new and joining tonight. I'm meeting Darragh in two mins," I say, not looking her in the eye. I don't want to see her giving me the once over with disgust.

"Okay. I'll buzz him and let him know you're here and he can sign you in. That way, you can have a free trial, just in case … just in case you don't want to come back." She is all sweetness and light, but with a touch of venom in her words.

Surprisingly, her assumption that I'll give up after tonight actually spurs me on to make sure I come back, just to piss her off.

The door opens and Darragh walks out. Well, I think it's Darragh. It looks like him, except he's covered in sweat, and his muscles are shiny and tight. Wow, he is gorgeous and he's my best friend. I am such a lucky girl!

"Hey, Kay," he says, walking over and hugging me. I take a sneaky peak at the blonde bimbette staring at us and I hug him back … tightly.

"Hey, babe," I say, looking in her direction. You look hot tonight." I blush. What made me say that?

He laughs. "Yeah, I'm sweltering." He turns to the blonde bimbette and says, "Kay is with me tonight. I don't have anyone else and I'll be leaving with her when we're done. Can you give me a form to fill in for her, please, Chelsea?" He smiles at her and she blushes, but instantly reaches for a clipboard.

"Here, Darragh. Have fun!" She rolls her eyes towards me, blatantly indicating that I will not be fun to be with tonight. She is really winding me up. I want to seriously smash her face in and I am not a violent person. Well, I might be if I have too much to drink. Well, not really.

He fills in the form and then grabs my hand. "You're coming with me, before you change your mind." He smiles at me. He really does know me.

"So, what's with bimbette on reception?" I ask,

before I kick myself for asking such a stupid question.

"What do you mean?" he asks, seeming genuinely confused.

"She was insinuating that I wasn't going to stay and that I wouldn't have fun. Who does she think she is to make those assumptions about me?"

What the hell is wrong with me tonight?

He stops and looks at me. Then he laughs. "Are you jealous?"

"What? Me? No way!"

"I think you are. She was nice to me, and looking at me and not you. I think you're jealous, Kay."

"Don't be stupid. What do I have to be jealous about? You do whatever you want and so do I. We're friends." Now I'm waffling, and I'm not sure I believe that myself.

"Hmm, if you say so," he says looking out of the corner of his eye at me. "Anyway, there's no stalling tonight. We need to work out what exercises are best for you, and how many times a week you need to be coming."

"You mean I have to come more than once a week?"

Why does that sound so rude to me? I think I

definitely need to get some sexual relief. I wonder if I can convince Maeve to come out with me this weekend and get drunk so I can have a shag.

He smiles then winks at me. "Of course you have to come more than once a week. It's no good just doing it once."

Now I blush even deeper. Then I realise he's playing with me.

"Fuck off, Darragh. Now tell me which exercises to do or I'm out of here. I've already broken into a sweat and I haven't done anything yet."

He laughs. Then he takes me into a room where there are some big, bouncy yoga balls, some weights, and floor to ceiling mirrors. All. Around. The. Fucking. Room.

"You have got to be shitting me, Darragh. I can't bend over or stretch in here and look at myself in the mirror. No fucking way!" I turn to walk back out the way I came in.

He grabs me and pulls me close to his body. My back is touching his chest and he has his arms wrapped around my waist. He walks me to the mirror and then stands there until I look up.

"Stay looking in that mirror, Kay. Look at yourself. See how beautiful you are. You have to feel that on the inside for you to be happy with yourself on the outside. Don't let your weight define you as a person. You should never have to make do with second best. You are beautiful." He is looking in the mirror into my eyes as he speaks.

I look down to the ground again but he puts his finger under my chin and lifts it so I'm looking in the mirror. He slowly unwraps his arms from around my waist and then he runs his hands down my sides. He pulls my t-shirt and twists it at the back, and I can see a little outline of a waist.

"Okay, let's be serious here, Kay. I want you to take pictures of yourself in black leggings and a tight black t-shirt when you go home. You don't have to show me the pictures, but keep them, and then in a couple of weeks, we can look at them and see if there is any difference. I will make a bet with you that if you keep coming to the gym and you keep on your fat club diet then there will be a difference. A noticeable difference."

"I don't believe you, but I'm never one to turn down a bet. What's the prize?" I say, turning to face him.

"I think we can come up with something between us. I'm sure there are some things you'd like me to do at home for you, and I'm sure there are a few things I'd like you to do for me."

I laugh. "Like what?"

"Well, there's ironing and cleaning for a start," he says, laughing.

"Let me tell you, there is no chance I'm cleaning your room after you have had bimbos in there!" I put my hands on my hips.

He laughs again. "I haven't had a bimbo in ages."

"Yeah, you did. I saw one leaving your room this weekend."

"Not mine you didn't. That must have been Shane's room."

I don't have the energy to argue with him. "Well, I'm sure we can work something out between us. Now tell me what I've got to do to change my shape!"

He chuckles and then takes me over to do some stretches. He writes them down on my card so I know what I need to do, and how many of them.

After we've done some stretching, he makes me watch him as he does some core exercises. He sits, or just about sits, on the yoga ball, with his feet planted evenly apart. Then he slowly leans back, not touching the ball, and then straightens up again. That looks easy.

After he's done ten of them, he makes me sit on

the one next to him. Well, that's easier said than done.

Attempt Number One.

I try to put a small part of my bum on the yoga ball, but it just rolls out from under me and I land flat on my bum.

Attempt Number Two.

I manage to sit on the edge of the ball with my feet spread evenly apart. Then, when I lean back, I must go too far because my feet have left the floor and the ball rolls so that my head hits the floor and the ball rolls away like a pinball machine.

Attempt Number Three.

Okay, I think I know how this works now. Third time lucky? Yay, the ball doesn't roll away from me. I don't fall off, but fuck me, my stomach hurts when I do it. It makes me want to puke.

———

After I've done ten of them, I sit up and look at Darragh, who is trying to hold his laugh in.

"Darragh, is it supposed to hurt this much? I want to puke!"

"No pain, no gain!" He laughs. "In all serious-ness, yes, it should hurt, especially to start with as you're pulling muscles that don't get used very often. It will get better."

"It better fucking do!" I say, grunting.

He puts his hand out for me to take and he pulls me up. "Right, let's do the next exercise." He pulls me over to the blue mats on the floor. "Sit down there, Kay." He points to the first mat and then he sits on the second one.

I sit down, not so gracefully as Darragh, then lay down. I'm knackered already!

He hands me a small ball and I roll it around in my hand as he grabs one for himself.

"Right, watch me and do what I do," he says. He's sitting up with his legs flat on the mat, out straight.

He then takes the ball and twists his upper body, and places the ball on the ground just behind his waist. Then he picks it up and twists, and places it on the ground on the other side. It means his upper body is twisting both ways.

I try it and realise it's quite easy.

"Keep your legs straight, Kay. Keep your back straight."

Okay, maybe it's not that easy. I know it sounds really easy and you're probably laughing and thinking that anyone can do it. Well, you give it a go and then tell me you think it's easy!

We do ten of those too, and then he stops, writing on my card again.

"Okay, we're going to lie down now," he says, lying down so he's flat on his back.

"Darragh, that is the best thing you've said all night!" I chuckle as I lie down flat.

"I'll see if you'll say that in a few minutes, Kay." He chuckles back.

I groan.

"Right, so lay with your back flat to the floor and then slowly lift your legs together. Keep them straight."

I do as he says and I can feel the stretch in my stomach as I lift my legs.

"Good girl. Now, keep them at that height and count to ten then lower them again. Count to ten again and then lift them. Do that ten times."

"Urgh, I am going kill you later, Darragh." I hold my legs for the count of ten, but can't wait to lower them. My legs are shaking so much when they're up in the air and I don't get any relief when they're back on the floor either.

"I feel sick. Darragh, I think I need to puke!"

He laughs. "This is only the warm up, babe."

I do all ten sets of the exercises and then try to sit up. It hurts. Not just my back, but also my stomach.

I eventually manage to sit up by lifting my legs really high and then swinging them down fast enough that my top part swings up and I end up sitting up. Have you ever done that when you're in bed? Yeah, I knew it. It's great when you have a bad back and need to sit up quickly!

He gives me another five exercises to do, and then he looks at me. My face is as red as a beetroot, and my hair is plastered to my face. Thank God we didn't do any cardio work.

"I think you've had enough for tonight, Kay. You did a great job, much better than I expected. I think you deserve a treat when we get home," he says, putting his arm around my shoulders.

I wriggle out of his hold. "Urgh, Darragh, no bad feeling, but I hate sweat on a bloke. Unless it's when he's balls deep inside me."

I turn and walk away. Realising what I just said makes me even redder. Oh my God, I want the floor to swallow me whole!

He laughs out loud and continues to laugh as he leads me to the changing room.

"Get your arse in there and have a shower and

then you can take me home. See you out the front in about fifteen minutes," he says, as he disappears into the changing room next to me.

I shake my head and walk into my changing room. I become extremely self-conscious as soon as I walk in. There are women in there who obviously don't care who sees them naked. I have my mouth open. Wow, they're just walking around with no clothes on and not even trying to cover themselves with a towel.

Well, I'm not ready to join this nudist club tonight, so I take myself into the nearest cubicle, take my clothes off, and wrap my body in a towel. No, make that a bath sheet. You know, those towels that can fit the whole family in? Then I head for the showers.

After finishing the shower and changing in the cubicle again, I walk out to meet Darragh.

He's leaning up against the wall, waiting for me, and I have to take a second glance at him. How did I end up with someone this good-looking as my best friend?

"Hey there, Kay. How are you after the shower?"

"Not sure. I think I feel good, but it's like a

sugar rush. It's going to crash very quickly, so let's get home."

He follows me out to the car, and while I'm driving home, he chats randomly about people coming to the gym.

"I just realised I didn't sign up for membership."

"It's okay. I sorted it for you."

"No, I meant a full membership, not just a guest membership for a night."

"Yeah, I signed you up for a full membership. I get discount, you know?"

"Did you really? Thanks, hun. I'll pay you back."

"I don't want you to pay it back. Just knowing you want to come means the world to me, Kay. Just make sure you keep coming back." He smiles at me.

When we get home, I go into the kitchen and start preparing my food for the next day. It's kind of a habit now, and not so much of a chore as before.

As I'm finishing up, I feel someone looking at me. Turning around, I see Shane leaning up against the door jamb.

"What are you staring at?" I ask him, with my arms folded.

"Just watching what you're doing. Those yoga pants really suit you, you know?"

I don't know whether he's joking or not. He isn't smiling or giving anything away.

"Thanks," I say, turning around and putting everything in the fridge.

"I'm proud of you, Kayleigh. Even going to the gym takes courage. You might just make it this time," he says, as he leaves the kitchen.

What does he mean by that? I might be able to stick to my diet? I might be able to lose weight? What the fuck?

5
DOUCHEBAG CENTRAL

If I thought I felt bad yesterday, it's nothing to how I feel today. I thought it was just the morning after exercising that was going to burn, but today, I'm positively on fire. My joints are stiff and my stomach hurts when I breathe, let alone when I laugh. Do I have to go again?

Guess what? It's Thursday, and yes, I do have to go again. Today. After work. I promised Darragh. I don't even know how I'm going to walk to my desk, let alone do some toning exercises. I'll kill him first!

As I'm leaning over the worktop in the kitchen, trying to take small breaths so they don't hurt, I hear someone walk in. I turn my head slightly. It's Darragh.

"Hey, Kay. How're you today?" he says with a smirk.

"You fucker. You made me believe it would be better today, not worse!"

"I don't think I did, but you know how to make it go away, don't you?" He winks at me.

Is he being suggestive with me?

"No, but you look like you're going to tell me. Are you offering?" I smile and try to look sexy.

"Yes, babe, I am offering. Tonight, seven o'clock, my gym. Be there and ready to do some more exercises. It's the only thing that will burn through the pain." He stands there, looking all smug.

"Bastard. I thought you were talking about something more interesting, like sex or something!"

"Well, that could work too." Now he's laughing out loud, then he suddenly stops and looks at me. I think he just realised that I thought he was offering to have sex with me to help the burn. "Oh. You thought…. Well, I'm up for it if you are. It might help too." He wiggles his eyebrows.

I stand there, open-mouthed, looking at him. "Fuck off!" I shout, as I see the smile on his face.

He comes up behind me and wraps his arms around my waist, leaning into my ear. "I would if you want me to. I'd love to see all your curves. I got a good look at them the other day in the gym, but it wasn't enough."

Laughing, I say, "I think you saw the best bits,

especially when I bent down and the lights went out!"

He laughs and pulls away. "You put yourself down too much, babe. You're sexy, and it's my mission to make you realise it. Now, get your sexy arse upstairs," he says, smacking it. "Make sure you pack your gym stuff. I'll see you at seven tonight." Then he leaves the house, leaving me with my mouth wide open, wondering what the hell just happened.

After packing my gym bag, I head to work and then to the gym afterwards. My exercises don't feel so bad tonight. Maybe I've pulled the muscles so much they aren't elastic anymore. Either that, or I've broken them, but the burn isn't so bad today.

We do a few more exercises tonight and then he says, "Well done, Kay. You've done fantastic. It's not as bad the second time around, huh?"

"I suppose not."

"Have the weekend off and then next week you can do a little bit of cardio."

"No freaking way!"

"Just a little, on the treadmill at a walking pace, or on the bike at your own pace. That's all. Nothing really strenuous."

"Okay, okay, okay, if it means you get off my back."

He chuckles. "Yeah, I promise I won't mention exercise again until Monday. Take the weekend off. Are you going out?"

"Thanks! Yeah, I'm going out tomorrow night. I might buy myself something new to wear. I haven't been out in ages and I need to feel good about myself."

He puts his arm around my shoulder and I can feel his sweat and smell his manly smell. It affects me in my core. I can't believe I'm having dirty thoughts about my housemate and best friend. That is so bad. I really need to pull this weekend. Blow them cobwebs off.

"Let me know where you go, I might bump into you."

"Okay. Not sure yet. I'll check with Maeve. I am going on the pull though, so don't cramp my style. You know what I'm saying?"

He laughs. "I wouldn't dare cramp your style, babe."

We head off to change and then go home. I don't see Shane tonight, so at least he can't be offensive.

Friday night rolls around. At lunchtime, I went out and bought a black dress to wear. I tried some clothes on the night before and they were a little looser. Nothing much, but it made me feel good, and made me want to buy something new to show off my curves. Darragh is right; I shouldn't hide from everyone. If I love myself and have confidence in myself then so will others.

Once I'm dressed and have my make up on, I take a look in the full-length mirror in my room. I had my hair put up after work and it looks gorgeous, even if I say so myself.

I twirl and smile at myself. "You are so going to get those cobwebs blown away tonight, girl!"

There's a knock at my door. "Kay, are you on the phone or something?" It's Darragh.

"No, I was just talking to myself. You can come in, I'm decent."

He walks in and does a double take, and then he comes over to me and stands behind me, looking in the mirror. He takes one of my hands and holds it up in the air so I can do a full twirl like a ballerina.

"Stunning. You are so going to get lucky tonight, babe."

I blush. I obviously don't see what he sees in my mirror. All I see is a big girl who is trying to look like a slim girl. However, I do look pretty, and that is what matters.

"Thanks, Darragh. I hope I get a lot of exercise so I don't have to worry about the number of calories I will be drinking tonight."

He laughs. It's only then I realise he is dressed to go out too.

"Where are you going tonight and with whom?" I ask, turning around to check him out.

"Just going out with my mates, that's all. Do you want to share a cab into town?"

"Yeah, great idea. Give me ten minutes, just to make sure I'm ready."

"No problem. See you downstairs in ten."

I check myself again in the mirror and spray some perfume. Then I smile and make my way downstairs.

———

A few hours later. "Oh my God, Maeve, what are we drinking? How many fat points are there in here?"

"I don't know, but I would guess about nine or ten."

"In each one? Shit, I've had at least five."

"Don't worry about it. You don't let your hair down often enough, hun," she says, bringing me the next drink.

We've been drinking cocktails since I met Maeve in town. I'm having a great time. I feel great. I've had some glances, nothing serious, but a few glances alright.

We walk onto the dance floor to make some serious shapes to the music. I love dancing; it makes me feel free. I can be sexy in the way I move, and I know I am. My confidence grows and I'm soon swaying my hips to the music, losing myself in time to the beat.

Maeve looks over my shoulder and smiles; she nods her head to the side. I slowly turn around using dance moves and see this good-looking guy watching me. He starts to sway his hips in time to the music behind me and I feel him coming closer to me. I turn and he slides in behind me. I like this. I could get used to this.

He runs his hands down my waist. Yes, I admit to pulling my stomach in as soon as I realise what he's doing. Then he pulls me closer so my back is touching his front.

"You're really sexy. You have some great moves. I bet you're amazing in bed with those moves," he says into my ear.

I can feel my heartbeat rising. Yes! Who's going to get lucky tonight? Yeah, that's right. Me! Kayleigh Davies. Sex goddess herself.

"Wouldn't you like to know?" I say back to him, twisting my neck so I can whisper in his ear. He uses the opportunity to kiss my neck.

I think I moan.

Next thing I know, his mate comes up to him and hands him twenty euro. "I never thought you would do it." He is laughing hysterically.

"I told you the fat girls are always more thankful for whatever they can get," the man behind me says.

I pull away. "You fucker! Who gives you the right to play with people like that?" I jab my finger into his chest.

"What? You must be desperate for some attention. I was only giving you what you wanted." He's sneering at me. God, when he looks like that he is so ugly. Inside and out.

"You deserve for your dick to fall off from some

disease." I jab him again. "Don't play with people's feelings. Karma is a bitch and you best remember that!"

He walks off laughing with his mate.

Maeve is at my side. "What the fuck just happened there?"

"Come on. Let's go to the toilet and I'll tell you." I grab her hand and pull her off the dance floor.

When we get to the bathroom, we both go into the same cubicle. That's what girls do, we always go to the bathroom in pairs and we always share a cubicle.

"What the fuck happened?" she asks.

I sit down on the toilet lid and sigh. "He was only dancing with me for a bet."

"No fucking way."

I nod. "Yes fucking way!"

It's not the first time it's happened to me, but it just brings home to me that even though I have lost some weight, admittedly not enough, I'm still considered fat.

"He said to his friend that fat girls are thankful for any cock they get."

"He did not say that?"

I nod. "Yes, he did. He's a bastard. I told him

karma is a bitch." I can feel a tear sliding down my face. Crap, now I'll have to retouch my foundation, otherwise it will look streaky.

She kneels in front of me. "Listen, Kay, he's a pig. You're better off you found out now what an arsehole he was before you slept with him. At least you made it out alive."

"Yeah, so did he. I was so ready to have sex that I think I would have killed him in bed."

Maeve laughs and I join her.

I walk out of the cubicle and look in the mirror. I can see my shape is changing, and a few more weeks at the gym and properly doing my diet, I know that I will look much better. I just need to persevere, and my friends are behind me so I know I can do it.

We leave the bathroom and walk out to the bar. "Let's get another drink," Maeve says, this time pulling me behind her.

"Actually, I think I've had enough. Can I just get a sparkling water or diet lemonade, please?" She looks at me then nods her head.

I turn to face the dance floor when someone touches me on the waist. "Hey, beautiful."

I've had enough of this. Who do these people think they are? "I've had enough of your bullshit for one night. Go pick on someone who cares." I turn around and see it's Darragh, so I hug him. "It's you."

He hugs me back. "What's going on, Kay?" I can feel him tense up so I pull back. He obviously doesn't like me hugging him in public. It annoys me a little, because at home he's all touchy feely, and then when we're out, he doesn't want to let other people see me touch him. What's going on?

"What do you mean?" I say, turning to face him.

"Why are you giving me abuse? Did you think I was someone else?"

"Yes, I did. Some guys think it's funny to pick on the fat girl and make her cry. I fucking hate this place. I think I need to go home." I turn to find Maeve to tell her I'm going home, when I feel a hand tighten around my wrist.

"Kay. I'll ask you again. What's going on?"

Maeve turns up and hands me my drink. "Some fucker decided it was a good idea to have a bet with his mates that he could get Kay to dance with him. He told her that the fat girls are always thankful for whatever they get."

Darragh is quiet for a minute then he lets rip. "Where is the fucker? No one talks about Kay like that." He starts looking around, but I don't know who he's looking for because he doesn't know who did it. "Where is he, Maeve?"

She looks around and all I want is for the ground to open up and swallow me.

I put my hand on his arm, trying to stop him. "Don't worry about it. I just want to go home now. I've forgotten all about it."

"No, Kay. These people can't say things like that and get away with it," Darragh says, taking my hand. "I've got your back, babe."

Maeve points out the guy to Darragh. "There, that's the dickhead."

He pulls me behind him and I can feel myself trying to slow him down, but he's like the world's strongest man pulling a Mini Cooper behind him. He will not be stopped until he reaches his destination.

When he gets up close to the guy, he puts his arm around my shoulder and taps the guy on the shoulder.

"Hey, excuse me."

The guy turns around, and when he sees me, he grins. His friend nudges him.

"What do you want? I didn't get far if you're looking for ideas." He laughs.

Darragh says, "I don't need ideas of what I'm going to do to this beautiful woman. I can't wait to sink my cock into her hot, tight pussy."

OH MY GOD. Did he just say that? I can feel the blush rising, and even though I know he's just saying it, I really want it. He is turning me the fuck on.

"Good luck with that," the guy says looking at the floor.

"I don't need luck. But just a word of advice, don't play with someone's feelings like that. It makes you an arsehole. This woman is gorgeous, and you will get your comeuppance one day. I think you'll be going home alone tonight because you're ugly on the inside. No one wants ugly."

'Who the fuck do you think you are?"

"I'm the one taking this beautiful woman to heaven and back." Darragh turns me and walks me away.

I hear the guy shout to him. "Well, don't go down on her because I hear it will be like looking over the top of a sliced loaf." His friends start laughing. God, they are arseholes.

Before I even notice, Darragh has moved. He has the guy pinned up against the nearby wall.

"Don't you dare talk to her like that ever again. Do you hear me?"

The guy must be scared because he just nods his head and looks over to me. "I'm … I'm sorry. I didn't mean it. We were just having a laugh."

I don't know what to say, but I pull Darragh off him. "Come on, babe. He's not worth it. Now tell me more about what you're going to do to me tonight," I say, but only to get the other guy's attention, of course.

I would love to know what Darragh would do to me if I ever made it into his bed.

"I want to devour every part of you," he says, as he moves closer to me. Then, before I can think about anything else, he kisses me. But it's like he hasn't eaten anything in days. He devours me and pulls me closer to him. His tongue is fighting with mine, and I can't keep my hands off him. It's like fireworks going off inside my body.

When he pulls away, he winks at me. "Does that give you an idea, Kay?" he says, turning to look at the guy one more time. "What about you? I bet you can see how beautiful she is now, right?"

He takes my hand and pulls me over to Maeve who is standing there with her mouth wide open. If this was a cartoon, her tongue would be running across the floor. She looks like she's drooling.

"What the fuck just happened? I was looking for you and I saw you headed over to that fucker and then … and then I saw the hottest kiss I have ever seen. My knickers are totally soaked after watching that. Kay, your knickers must be on fire."

For one moment, I thought Darragh was my man, that he wanted me as much as he told that guy he did. Maeve just brings me back to reality and makes me realise that Darragh did that to get back at that guy for talking shit about me, not because he really wants to sink his cock into me.

I grab my glass, and even though it's just water, I chug it back. "I think I want to go home. Sorry, Maeve. I need to get out of here." I turn and storm off to get my coat from the cloakroom and head out to find a taxi.

Maeve runs after me. "Wait, Kay. I'll come with you."

"You don't have to. Honestly, I'll be fine."

"I know I don't, but I want to," she says, grabbing my arm and walking to the taxi with me.

It's only when we're sitting in the taxi that she says, "So… how long have you been crushing on Darragh?"

"I don't know what you're talking about," I say, looking out of the window.

"Yes you do."

"He instigated the kiss you know, not me," I say, indignantly.

"I know that! But your reaction afterwards proves you have a crush on him."

"Maeve, I didn't realise it myself until after he kissed me. I wanted him to want me. You should have heard what he said to that guy. He told him that he was going to go home and sink his cock into my tight pussy. I wanted that so much, it hurt. I know that he will never want me in that way, and it hurts."

"How do you know he doesn't want you? He touches you all the time. He looks at you all the time. He kissed you extremely passionately. I thought I was going to have an orgasm just watching. He likes you. When are you going to open your eyes and see that?"

"Look at me, Maeve. Just look at me. All of me. I'm fat! Not skinny like his usual type. I never will be. Even if I diet and exercise every day, I will never be skinny. How could he want me?"

She sighs heavily. "There's no point talking about it now. You won't listen to me anyway. I'm going to stay with you tonight and then we can talk more tomorrow."

"You don't need …."

"I know I don't need to, but I want to. Now, come on. Do you know how many men wanted a bit of me tonight? Loads, so think yourself lucky." She laughs.

I laugh along with her. "Just so you know, I'm not into lady love or anything." Then we both fall about the place laughing.

When we get out at my house, the light is on in the kitchen and I hope it's not Darragh. It's not, it's Shane. Now I wish it was Darragh.

"Look what the cat dragged in," he says, eyeing us both up and down. "Looking good, ladies." He looks at me. "Especially you, Kay. I didn't think you would stick with the diet, but I have to say that I can tell it's working. A few more weeks and you will be seriously hot!"

"Fuck off," I say, as I push past him and 'accidentally' hit him with my shoulder on the way past. He stumbles and then laughs.

Maeve and I get undressed and climb into bed. We talk for about twenty minutes and then I fall asleep. I have strange dreams when I drink and I don't sleep well. I'm always awake super early after a skin full.

Tonight is no different, except I dream of Darragh, of course.

I feel him right beside me, kneeling on the floor. "Babe," he whispers. "Kay."

I don't say anything, just lay there, looking into his face. God, he's so handsome.

"Kay, I meant what I said. I want to do everything I said. You just don't believe me." I feel him kiss me on my lips as I stare into his eyes. My lips don't move; it's like I'm a stone statue looking out at him.

He runs his hand over my face and kisses me again. "I want you, babe. I'll wait forever if I have to. I just want you and no one else."

He gives me one final peck on the lips then he stands up and leaves my room. I can't even reach out my hands to stop him. It's like he's slowly slipping away from me.

———

In the morning, I have a headache. It's throbbing and I feel shattered. When I roll over to look at the ceiling, Maeve wakes up too. We lie side by side, not saying anything.

After a while, we march downstairs to get some

coffee; I really need some today. "Oh, God. Give me that coffee now. When do you think they will invent something that will turn on when I think about it?"

Maeve laughs. "I don't know babe, but when they do, I want one too."

"I turn on when you think about me," Darragh says, leaning up against the door. "Wait, sorry, no. I get turned on when I think of you." He smiles his megawatt smile.

"Fuck off, Darragh. I don't need your smart mouth today." I turn back around to hide the blush that is creeping up my face.

He chuckles. "So, what are you two lovely ladies doing today?"

I spin around and surprise myself more than them when I say, "I'm off to the gym today. I need to get in shape. I don't want anything like last night happening to me again. Fat Kayleigh is on the high road and she won't be back!"

"Kay, stop torturing yourself. Don't listen to what one arsehole said. He was talking shit!" Maeve says, shaking her head.

"Yeah, don't listen to him. Then again, if you are going to the gym, I can come with you and we can train some more," Darragh says, smiling.

Do I want to train with Darragh? Hell yeah!

Will I be able to stop my filthy thoughts coming to the forefront of my mind? Hell no!

Will I get turned on if he touches me again? Absobloodylutely!

Fuck it; you only live once, right?

"Sounds like a good idea to me. I'm sure I can wear you out," I say, sounding braver than I really am.

"Great. We can do some cardio today. I'll put you on the treadmill and then the bike and cross trainer."

I roll my eyes at Maeve. "Are you coming?"

She shakes her head and laughs. "No freaking way. I am off to nurse this hangover and get ready to do it all again tonight."

"I'm not going anywhere tonight. I'm not drinking for a while. I need to really get this diet kick started."

"Are you sure, Kay?" she says, looking worried. I can in her eyes that she thinks I am only doing this because of that stupid arse last night. In a way I am, but really I'm doing this for me. I don't want to feel that way again.

"Yeah. I need to do this for myself, not for anyone else."

She gives me a kiss and then grabs her stuff and leaves with a promise to ring me later on.

Darragh looks at me. "Are you sure you're doing this for the right reasons, Kay?"

I smile at him. I know for sure that I am. "I am absolutely sure, Darragh. I know what I want!"

"Right then. Let's go."

6
TWO MONTHS LATER

"Come on, Kay. Push harder. Come on, babe. You know you like it. Harder," Darragh says, as he pushes against my legs.

I push as hard as I can and I can see him starting to falter; he looks like it's going to be over soon. He's sweating, red in the face, and a big smile comes over my face as I take a deep breath and bear down for the last time.

He falls back as my feet push his body away from me. Landing on the floor, he smiles. "Well done, Kay. You did it. You finally did it."

I laugh. I've been trying to have the strength in my legs to push him over for the last two months. It has been hard work and taken sheer determination, but I finally did it.

Oh, right! Did you think we were having sex? Oh my God, that is so funny. No, we're in the gym, as usual! Since that awful night, I've become obsessed with my diet and the gym. I'm feeling healthier and more confident in myself. Now, don't get me wrong, I'm not a gym bunny, but I have finally realised that I'm never going to be a slim size ten.

I stand over him and put my hand out to help him up, and I surprise myself by being able to help him up easily.

"I'm so proud of you, Kay," he says, pulling me into a hug. "I know you've wanted to do that for a long time. I knew you would get there."

He puts his arm around my shoulder and walks me back to the changing room. "See you in a bit." He kisses me on the side of my head and we go into our separate rooms

Grabbing my shower gel and shampoo, I walk over and jump in the shower. It's funny, before I lost this weight, I would never have got into a public shower, but now, I don't care if people look at me. I'm happy with who I am, and that's all that matters.

When I've dressed and dried my hair, I walk out to the reception to find Darragh leaning up against the desk, talking to the receptionist. I watch them for a minute. She's staring at him, smiling, blinkered to everything around her. He smiles at her, but he isn't returning her flirtatious looks. He's changed a lot over the last two months. Well, actually, when I think about it, he's changed over the last six months. I don't see him flirting with girls. I don't see any coming out of his room on a Sunday afternoon doing the walk of shame.

He sees me and smiles. "Come on then, slave driver," he says. "Let's get home. You've got somewhere to be tonight and you can't be late."

I say goodbye to the receptionist, who looks me up and down in disgust. To her, I am still fat, but that's fine. I don't want to be like her anyway. I am me! I want to be like … me!

An hour and a half later, I hear, "Right, Kayleigh. Step up on those scales. How do you think you did this week?" She smiles at me as she takes my book, which is covered in Fat Club bling.

She opens the book, smooths her hand over it, and looks up to me, smiling.

I don't take everything off now to weigh myself. I don't need to. I am what I am.

"This week has been great. I've been to the gym and prepared everything, so I'm hoping that I've met my next milestone. I think there's room for one more piece of bling on there." I laugh as I step on the scales

She starts clapping her hands and has the

biggest smile on her face. "Well done, Kayleigh, you've lost five pounds this week. You've made the next milestone. I'm so proud of you." She starts writing my weight down and then says, "I'm going to give this to Sophie and she will give you your bling. Well done!"

"Seriously? That's fantastic. I'm so happy." I can't wait to text Maeve and Darragh. We're having a treat tonight. We're going to have an Indian take-away I haven't had one in over two months and I'm looking forward to it.

Sitting waiting for the others to weigh in, I text Maeve first.

Kayleigh: Hey hun, I've done it. I lost five pounds this week. I am on a freaking roll baby.
Maeve: Oh my god I am so proud of you, well done. I'll be at yours by the time you get back and we can celebrate.
Kayleigh: We sure will, I am going to savour every taste, flavour and smell of this curry tonight.
Maeve: See you later
Kayleigh: I did it! I freaking did it! Thank you so much for your help, you've been great.
Darragh: Well done, you rock do you know that?

You were determined to do it and you've managed it. So proud of you right now. xx
Kayleigh: Thanks, can't wait for tonight x
Darragh: Me neither xx

Looking up, I notice that Sophie has started the class and then she starts to give out the bling.

"So, our next milestone achiever is Kayleigh. Five pounds lost this week and never to be seen again." Everyone starts clapping and I can feel my face getting flushed. She continues, "Kayleigh has been with us for a few months, and at first, it was hard work and she could have easily dropped out of the group and given up. In fact, she has done many times before. For some reason, this time it was the right time for her and she has lost an amazing three stone in the process." Again, everyone starts clapping.

I go to speak, to say something, but she holds her hand up. "Kayleigh, we want you to share your journey with us and explain to the rest of the group the ups and downs of how you have got to this point. Are you okay with that?"

I look around the group and see women of many ages, nationalities, and shapes. If my journey can motivate other women to lose weight and be more confident in themselves, then who am I to stop them?

I tell them how I got to this point. I even tell them about the club with that arsehole and how that was my turning point. That was the point when I realised I didn't just want to be on the fringe of society anymore. I had more to give than that. I also admit that it has become an obsession; dieting and toning up. I don't go drinking anymore, I don't go clubbing anymore. All I ever seem to do it count the fat points of everything that passes my lips.

Telling them about these things makes me realise that I have become obsessed, and it isn't healthy. I need to find a proper balance between dieting, tonight, and living my life. So I tell them about the Indian I'm having tonight. They laugh, and Sophie starts shaking her head. I laugh too.

"So, even though I have enjoyed this journey, I know that I can't afford to lose any more weight because I won't be me anymore. I am heavy boned. I am bigger than some of you just starting out, but I am me! And do you know what? I love me!"

They all clap and I feel some tears running down my face. These people have become family over the last few months. These are the people I turn to when I need the motivation to carry on, when I don't know what to eat when all I feel like is a big, dirty, burger and chips from the chipper. They've kept me on track as much as I have.

Sophie hands me my book, and I have a big sense of pride when I see all the glitzy stickers on the front. There is no more room, and I know that, even though I will be relaxing a little on my diet, I won't be back.

After class, I drive home, and Darragh and Maeve are there already. They have ordered and set the table, I notice there's a bottle of wine open too. Smiling, they hug me and we all start talking at once.

"Shut the fuck up. I just want to sit down and savour every flavour of this food," I say, sitting down and starting to put everything I can on my plate. I know I won't eat it all, my stomach has shrunk so it can't take it all, but I love looking at the food; it looks gorgeous.

We don't speak for about fifteen minutes while we all eat, then I hear myself moaning, "God, this is amazeballs. Oh, God."

Maeve starts laughing, "Jesus, Kay, you sound like you're having an orgasm."

"I wish. This is a foodgasm that I'm having right now. This is much better than sex!"

"Not with the right person it's not!" Darragh says, winking at me.

"Is that right?"

"Yeah, that's right." He stares at me and I stare back at him, then he reaches over the table and takes my hand.

Maeve starts choking on her food, but we don't look at her, we just keep looking at each other. It's like she isn't even here, although I can hear her. She's making lots of noises, and I think I see her face going a bit red.

"Help here!" she shouts, and finally we turn to look at her. She is red in the face. There are tears running down her face from coughing so much.

"Jesus, Maeve, are you okay?" I say, banging her on her back.

Whatever it is passes and then she takes the glass of water Darragh fetched her.

"You fuckers! I could have choked to death and all you two could do was stare into each other's eyes. Just fuck already!"

"What do you mean?" I ask, blushing.

"You two have been eyeing each other up for the last six months. Just admit your feelings and get this pent up sexual frustration out of the way. It's getting really awkward being in your company." She has her hands on her hips and is staring at us.

When I look at Darragh, he's smiling. "You know she's right, Kay. I've told you often enough how much I want you."

For a minute, I think I'm in an alternative reality and he said he wants me. ME! Kayleigh Davies, fat girl.

"Why? because I lost weight?" I ask, offended.

"For fuck's sake, Kay," Maeve says. "Darragh has wanted you for a very long time. I told you that. Way before you lost weight. Isn't that right, Darragh?"

He looks at me and takes one of my hands in his. "Yeah. I've wanted you since I moved in here. You've always been beautiful to me. I've told you loads, but you never wanted to believe me. Your size doesn't matter to me, but I've been so happy to be a part of your journey, Kay." He kisses my hand.

"You … you liked me when I was bigger?" I stumble over the words.

"Yes. I see your beauty inside and out. You've always been beautiful, you just needed to see it for yourself," he says, staring into my eyes.

"Right, time out!" Maeve says, making a 'T' with her hands. "I want to finish my dinner, without choking, and then I'm going to leave you two to discuss your, erm, future relationship."

"Sounds like a plan," I say, not even looking at her.

We're all silent while we eat, and every one of us is rushing to finish. Maeve leaves about fifteen minutes later, and as soon as I've watched her get into her car, I close the door. Darragh is right behind me, and when I turn, I bump into his chest.

He pushes me gently into the wall. "Stop me if you don't feel this connection we have, Kay. I want you, but I don't want to lose your friendship. You mean more to me than that." He is searching for something in my eyes.

I grab hold of his t-shirt and pull him closer to me. "Shut the fuck up and kiss me like you did in the club."

So he does.

EPILOGUE
ONE YEAR LATER

"Come on, Kay! Hurry the fuck up!" Maeve is shouting up the stairs to me. "We can't be late; we have to be there on time. You don't want to keep Darragh waiting, do you?

"I'm coming, hold your horses, girl." I laugh. No, I don't want to keep Darragh waiting. This is a special day. I've been planning this for months and I can't believe the day is finally here.

Climbing into Maeve's car, I'm really excited. My hands are sweaty, I try to tuck them under my thighs so that I don't keep moving them around. I can feel the whole of my body tensing with nerves. I never thought I would be able to do this, especially not with Darragh. I smile when I think of him. God was certainly looking down on me the day he brought Darragh into my life. When he kissed me that night, I forgot about everything. I had wanted him as much as he had wanted me, but I kept pushing him away. I'm glad I didn't push him away that night, or we wouldn't have ended up where we are today.

Shane moved out not long after we got together. He said he was sick of hearing our *sexscapades*. We didn't mind as, between us, we could afford the rent anyway. He moved into my room that first night. We both knew that our connection was something that wasn't going to change. We have been inseparable since.

I have put on a little bit of weight, I admit, but in my defence, a lot of that is muscle mass. I love going to the gym. Now that is a statement I never thought I would say. But I do. I like the way it makes me feel and the way it makes me look.

Not to mention the fact that Darragh is my personal trainer, and when he touches me, he sets me on fire. He touches me a lot at the gym. He touches me a lot anywhere, to be honest. I love his touch.

We have been training a lot recently; I wanted to be in shape for today. I want to look good. This is a big milestone for me and I intend to enjoy every minute of it.

We're getting closer, and my nerves are heightened by the fact that I know I will be seeing Darragh in ten minutes or so. He stayed with some friends last night. I missed him, but I know it won't be long before I see him again.

We pull into the car park and I see Darragh's car. My heart beats erratically with excitement. "There he is," Maeve says, pointing to a guy who is standing in the middle of the car park, looking around everywhere.

I get out of the car and run over to him. "Darragh, I can't believe it's time." I jump into his arms and he kisses me very indecently considering we're in public. When he lowers me down, he smiles at me.

"Babe, you look gorgeous, as usual. I missed you last night."

"I missed you too," I say, kissing him on the lips.

"For God's sake, you two. You would think you haven't seen each other for weeks or something, not just one night," Maeve says, laughing.

Darragh smiles and takes my hand. "Come on, girls. Let's get this over with and then we can tick it off our bucket list."

We go over to the registration desk. There are three people sitting there, smiling at us, and they take our names. "Here's your numbers. Have fun!" the lady says, smiling at us as we turn around to see about ten people covered in mud stumbling across the finish line.

Darragh looks at Maeve and me, smiles, and says, "Are you ready to get dirty, girl?"

We both nod, not really sure what we got ourselves into.

"Hell & Back, are you ready for us?" he shouts, and we set off.

Oh my God, did you think we were getting married? Ha ha, no, I've always been jealous of all those people who had enough stamina to do Hell & Back. I've always wanted to do it but didn't have the confidence.

As we get up to the starting line, we're ushered into a group or 'wave' as they call the groups of people who leave together. We then have to go through a very strenuous warm-up. Thank God I've been training or else I would have passed out already.

And we're off!

We run for a few kilometres before we get to the first obstacle – 'The Ice Baths'. There is a row of tyres over huge vats of icy water, with ice in it too.

"Oh my God, it's fucking freezing!" I shout to no one in particular.

"Come on, Kay, just keep moving, don't stop.

You stop, you get colder. Move!" Darragh pushes me on.

Next is the 'Square Net', which is basically a square climbing net elevated slightly, but to make it harder, there is a net above the net and you have to crouch down to climb through. My back is killing me.

After that we come to the 'Pipes'. We have to slide down these quite small, pipes. At the end is a huge mud bath which comes up to my knees. The pipe is disgustingly dirty, cramped, smelly, and freezing. Darragh goes first and helps to pull Maeve and me out of the pipes. He unceremoniously dumps us in the mud bath.

The next obstacle is the 'Monkey Bars.' Sounds easy, right? Wrong! We are freezing. Muddy. Tired. And we have to suspend over another mud bath and move our hands to carry us over to the other side. Again, Darragh gets there first and helps the two of us over.

We walk to the next obstacle which, I notice, is starting to go up a hill. The 'A Frame' is another net that we have to climb over, but this one goes up the side of a hill. Again, it's all muddy and slippery. Not easy to climb on.

I laugh when I see what's next on the agenda.

'Sack Attack'. It reminds me of being at the school sports day. We have to climb into a sack each and jump our way to one point and then back down the hill again. It's hard and I hurt everywhere.

On our way to the next obstacle, Maeve shouts out, "Why the fuck did I let you talk me into this, Kay? Did I tell you that I hate you right now?"

"I hate myself right now too. Why did I talk myself into it? Darragh, what the fuck are we doing this for?"

He laughs. "You were the one who wanted to do it. You even signed Maeve and me up when we weren't there. This one is all on you, babe. Enjoy it, this is some achievement and I'm proud of both of you," he says as he starts to crouch for the next obstacle.

'Wheely Tyred' is a low frame that has tyres suspended from it. We have to crawl through it and get through the tyres. There are so many people under the frame, it's like a traffic jam. I just need to keep pushing my way through. My back is killing me and I need to get out of here.

I stand and stretch my back as we make our way to 'The Swamp.' Yeah, you heard that right – a fucking swamp. There are ropes across the top of the swamp and I can see people are waist or chest deep in the slimy mud. This isn't like the mud baths though. This is thick, slimy, mud that you sink in and get stuck. I see people losing shoes and everything in the swamp.

Darragh helps me get through, and I help Maeve. These two mean so much to me, and it's our strong relationship that is getting us through these obstacles.

"I just want to lie down," I say, crouching down. "Please. Just for one minute."

Maeve comes up behind me. "No. Come on, Kay. You can do this. You can lie down when you get home. Not much further now."

She pulls me upright and we run to the next obstacle, 'cos I can't wait – yeah, right!

'Hell Slide' – okay, this can't be too bad, right? It's a slide. By definition, a slice is something that goes down and propels you forward. This slide does that alright. You have to dive onto it and then it is a near vertical drop of white tarpaulin what is covered in water and mud, and as you build up the momentum to the bottom, you slide into a mud bath before you can even take a breath.

"Oh my God, that was so much fun! Can I just do this obstacle all day? Please?" I say, pleading with the two of them as they reach the bottom behind me.

Maeve can't stop laughing. "That was hilarious! I don't think I've ever come down a slide so fast in my life."

Darragh comes up behind us and puts his hand on the bottom of our backs. "Come on, girls. The quicker we do this, the quicker we get drinking to celebrate."

He pushes us to the next obstacle. After going through a couple more obstacles, like another mud swamp and the river where you have to hold on to a rope and pull yourself against the running water, we arrive at the woods. I see people ahead of me running and screaming.

"Fuck, Darragh. How did I talk you into bringing me to do this?" I say, waiting at the bottom of the hill with my hands on my hips.

"I didn't, babe. So, if anyone should be mad, it's me and Maeve." He kisses me. "Come on. Not long now."

———

We run up the hill, holding hands, all three of us,

and as we get part way up, I feel a blinding pain on my leg. "Fuck! What was that?"

Darragh laughs. "Babe, this is 'Sniper Alley'. They're shooting you with little pellets."

Maeve screams next. "Fuck that!" she says, as she lets go of my hand and runs like I've never seen her run.

"Run, Forrest! Run!" I shout after her. She turns and gives me the two fingers. I start laughing, until I get another sting from another pellet.

I start running for my life, thinking I'm never going to get out of here.

When we get to the top of the hill, we stand and take a few deep breaths. I can see the finish line. I'm going to do this.

The last obstacle is called 'For Goodness Shocks,' and it is a net close to the ground that you have to crawl under. However, there are electric cables hanging down that give you small shocks as you touch them. There is no way to avoid them. I take a deep breath and just go for it. I hear lots of swearing from behind me, and in front of me, but I hear the most coming out of my own mouth. My mother would kill me if she could hear the language I'm shouting right now.

We make it through and then I hear Maeve shouting, "Oh my God! I can see the finish line."

"Where?" I can't see straight right now. My head feels like it's going to explode. I'm so cold.

"There, you nutter!" She points to the right. I see it.

"Come on, girls. Not far now. We can all do this. Let's hold hands and go over the line the way we came in, together." Darragh says, taking my hand and then taking Maeve's.

We run as fast as we can with our wet, muddy clothes, wet runners, and tired lungs.

As we get under the banner saying *finish line*, a camera flashes, and at that moment, I am the happiest I've been in a long time. I'm so happy, I start crying.

"What's the matter, babe?" Darragh asks. "Are you hurt?" he asks, running his hands over my body.

"No, but you will be if you keep doing that." I wink at him.

He laughs. "There's enough time for that later."

He takes the two of us into his arms and we have a group hug. It feels amazing to have achieved what I would never have dreamed of doing.

We go to the communal showers to wash some

of the dirt off so we can put some clean, warm clothes on.

"Oh my God. I've got mud in places where I didn't even know I had places." I laugh.

"Don't talk to me. I don't how we will get this mud off," Maeve says, laughing.

When we've cleaned up, we start to make our way back to the car, talking loudly about the whole experience.

"So, what did you like best?" Maeve asks.

"None of it. I hated it all," I say, trying to think whether I enjoyed anything at all. "Actually, passing the finish line was the best part for me."

She laughs. I look over to Darragh; he didn't answer the question

"Darragh., what did you…? Are you okay?" I say, stumbling over to him. He's on the floor. "Did you hu…"

He stops me. "I'm fine. Honestly. I just got a stitch." He rubs his stomach and then I see his hand disappear under his t-shirt and he flashes me his muscles. I smile, then his hand disappears lower into his shorts.

"For God's sake, Darragh, stop it. People can see you, you know?"

He chuckles then says, "Kay, I love you. You know that, right? I think I tell you often enough."

I laugh. Yes, he does. He's always telling me.

"You inspire me so much," he says. I point my finger at my chest and raise my eyebrows. He nods. "Yes, you. You've overcome so much over the last couple of years and you've changed yourself inside and outside, but MY Kayleigh is still in there. You didn't lose who you are along the way. I can't imagine my life without you in it."

I have tears in my eyes. He's so romantic.

"I want you to be my forever. Will you marry me and make me the happiest man alive?"

Maeve starts squeaking and jumping up and down. I stand there looking at him with my mouth wide open.

"Well? Will you?"

I realise I haven't answered it. "I might have to think about that. You might have to lose some weight first."

"KAY!" he says, looking at me.

"Yes! Of course, yes," I say, laughing and crying at the same time.

He jumps up, and that's when I notice he has a ring in his hand. He takes my left hand and slides the ring onto my ring finger. It fits perfectly.

"Oh my God. Darragh, it's beautiful. Did you pick this yourself or did you have help?" I ask, looking at Maeve.

"I picked it myself. You don't think I told Maeve, do you?" He laughs. "She can't hold her piss."

"Oi, you!" Maeve says.

"Sorry, babe," he says to her. "You know you would have started dropping hints as soon as you found out."

She comes over and gives us a group hug. "Yeah, you're right. I would."

This is now my newest happiest moment of my life.

I know Darragh says he fancied me when he first met me, and I really do believe him, but if I hadn't lost weight then we wouldn't have done Hell & Back and lots of other sports and fun. I wouldn't have been physically able to do half of the stuff we do now, so losing the weight was the best thing to happen to me, after Darragh, of course.

The diet and training doesn't define me. If I want to eat burger and chips then I will. I know that as long as I don't slack on my training then I can eat and drink when I want to. But do you know what? I don't like binging on food and drink anymore. I don't need the natural high it used to give me. I have something more addictive in my life now. Darragh!

My life after losing has definitely improved!

THE END

Keep clicking for sneak peaks of two more Krissy V books ….. Hunter and Whiskey

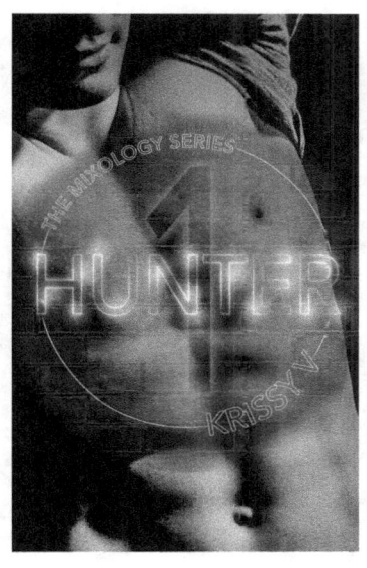

PROLOGUE

I am trashed. Totally and utterly fucked. I need to stop drinking as I can't really see much of what is going on around me. My bed is beckoning me. Stumbling around the lounge, I look for Grace, but I can't see her. She must be waiting for me upstairs.

There are bodies everywhere. Some of them have passed out and I know I will find them in the same place tomorrow when I'm eventually able to climb out of bed. I love University parties. They're crazy fun. Everyone gets absolutely trollied and has a fantastic time. No one cares what state they're going to be in the next day. College life is living the dream.

Staggering up to my room, I see some more people laid on the stairs, kissing each other. I think I just saw a couple who were attempting to have sex on the stairs. Looks interesting; I might have to suggest that to Grace one night when we're on our own.

Finding my bedroom, I grab hold of the door handle and open the door with a flourish, expecting to see Grace in bed waiting for me. What I see, however, is Grace in bed, but not waiting for me. She is laid on top of the bed naked and she's trying to undress another guy and drag him down on top of her.

I see RED. My head starts throbbing, my eyes glaze over and I can feel my heartbeat pulsing in my ears. I just want to punch whoever the fuck is leaning over Grace right now.

"What the fuck is going on here? Grace, what are you doing? I don't fucking believe you." I stumble into the room, feeling a lot more sober than when I opened the door.

Grabbing the guy who is standing by the bed, I yank him around to face me.

When I see who it is, I almost collapse on the floor.

"What the fuck, Coop?" I shout in his face.

"This is not what it seems like, Hunter. You have seriously got the wrong end of the stick."

"Are you fucking kidding me? You're meant to be my best friend and that is *my* girlfriend, not yours." I swing for him and knock him flat on the ground. Then I jump on top of him and keep punching him. I don't want to stop until he is dead. I'm angry, hurt and feel so let down. Coop and I have been friends for years. We were so happy when we got our results at school and realised that could go to the same University. It just made the whole University experience so much better.

Eventually someone hears the commotion and comes into my bedroom and drags me off him.

"Get the fuck out of here! Get out of my life and take that piece of trash with you." I shout, pointing at Grace. "I don't want to see either of you ever again. I don't even know who you are anymore and I don't fucking care. You mean nothing to me, neither of you."

He leaves the room and Grace tries to make me look at her. "Hunter, I love you! I don't know what happened. I was laid on the bed waiting for you and he came in and started touching me. I didn't do anything, I promise."

"Get the fuck out, Grace. I don't share and I *never* take sloppy seconds. I can't believe you betrayed me like this. I NEVER want to see you again. Fuck off!"

Dragging her out of the bed, I throw her clothes at her and almost push her out of the room.

Slamming the door behind the two of them, I throw myself down on the bed. If I never see either of them again in my lifetime, it will be too soon.

I swear to myself that I will never get into the position of loving someone and trusting another woman in my life. I intend to stay single and ready to mingle forever. I have my family and don't need anyone else. I'm going to look out for number one from now on. No one will ever be able to hurt me again.

BLOW JOB

1/2oz Baileys, ½ Oz Kahlua, Whipped Cream On Top

I hate my job, I really do. I have to serve cocktails to beautiful women all night. All I want to do is fuck them all night long, but I only get to take one home. Except for that one time....

Anyway, I can't dwell on that night because I need to live in the here and now.

Tonight is the first of our singles nights. Everyone thinks this is done for our customers, but if the customers don't pull anyone then we get to take them home... or the bathroom... or the cellar. You get the picture, right?

So, this is the outline of the night's activities. They come in, register, and get a free signature cocktail. Then they mingle and get more free cocktails. Well, they're not really free as they have to pay a registration fee, but they think they're free and that's what counts.

Tonight's cocktail is actually called a "Blow Job," which is technically a quick shot for most people, but my signature speciality of Bailey's, amaretto, and whipped cream is not one that goes down the hatch very quickly. Actually, the slower the better.

"Are you ready, Hunter?" Eddie asks as I'm wiping down the bar. Eddie is one of the barmen who works in Mixology. He's been here since we opened and was my best mate at school.

"As always, mate!" I smile. The anticipation of

all these single women is making me. I can't wait to see who comes through the door. "I have everything in order and ready to go in the cocktail booth. All we need now is the sexy ladies!"

He laughs. "That's all you think of - your cock!"

"Too right, Ed. What else is there to think of?"

He shakes his head. He's married and is no longer my wingman. "What about everlasting love? Feeling protective of someone and not wanting to be apart from them?"

I laugh. "Does that really exist?"

"Yeah. That's how I feel about Cindy. When I met her, I thought she was a one night stand, but she was like a drug. Now I hate being apart from her," he says, shaking his head.

"That's never gonna happen to me, mate. Not when I've got pussy on tap here." I hold my hands up to show him how much I've got. "No way!"

"Are you two ready?" Ainsley shouts as she stands at the door, ready to open up to the long queue of singletons outside. Ainsley is my sister and she manages Mixology so I can create the cocktails. She can be a little bit of a tyrant, but I love her.

Even though Mixology is my bar, my family makes it. Looking around the place, I see Skylar, my youngest brother, with his laptop, ready to beat out the tunes; Keaton, my closest brother, is manning the main bar with Ed; Zac, the middle brother, is at the door, ready to attack if anyone steps out of line, and Ainsley is staring at me, waiting for my thumbs up.

Smiling at her, I hold my thumbs up so she knows to open the doors and let the customers in.

———

Two hours later, we already know the night has been a success. The ladies are drunk, the men are prowling, and I've got a pocket full of phone numbers. One lady in particular has caught my attention - Bianca.

"Hey, Bianca," I say, looking at her name badge. When the customers register, they have to wear a name badge to make it easier to talk to each other. "How's your evening? Seen any men that tickle your fancy?" I wiggle my eyebrows at her.

"Yeah, definitely," she says, licking her lips, staring at me.

"How about I give you a Mixology special Blow Job? It's tonight's special cocktail... but with a twist," I say, looking her up and down.

She has long blonde hair, a sexy figure all

trussed up in a red patent dress, and I'd safely say she's not a virgin. She looks at me through her lashes and says, "I want one of your special Blow Jobs."

Grinning, I know it will be more than just her who wants one when they see what I have to offer.

"Coming right up, babe." Mixing the shot, I take my top off, to her complete surprise. Her eyes open wider and I hope her legs will open like that for me later.

Climbing up on the bar, Keaton starts cheering and Ed rolls his eyes. Lying down, I know everyone is watching what is unfolding on the cocktail bar.

"I think I'm going to like this," she says, licking her lips.

"I know you are, but not as much as I am!" I say gruffly.

I put the shot in between my legs as her eyes open wide. She slowly lifts her head from my crotch to my face and her eyes change colour, they become hooded and then they sparkle. She smiles at me and then licks her lips. She wants me.

"Take it, babe. Show me what you're gonna do to me later."

After being lifted on the bar by Keaton, she puts her hands on either side of my thighs and I can feel the heat radiating off them. She then, very slowly, leans down and starts licking the shot.

"Babe, don't spill any on my trousers. The aim is that you get the shot all drunk before lifting the glass up. You've got to suck hard."

She gasps. "I can do that."

I really hope she can.

She leans down again and I can feel her hot mouth wrapped around the glass, touching my now erect cock.

She sucks really hard like she's hoovering it up; it's really fucking sexy. When she's finished, she takes the glass in her mouth and lifts it up to a cheer from the watching crowd. Sitting up, I take the glass out of her mouth with mine and the bar goes even more mental. There are cheers and wolf whistles, and she blushed.

A wave of lust runs through me.

She wipes the back of her hand across her mouth as she had some cream left over. It's really sexy and I can't wait for her to wipe her mouth like that after I come down her throat.

Jumping back down behind the bar, everyone starts asking me for a Blow Job. I can't deny that it makes me feel good, but I don't do any more specials… that one was just for Bianca.

Feeling her watching me, I turn and face her. "When's your break, Hunter?" Everyone knows my name, so it doesn't surprise me when she uses it.

I smile. "In twenty minutes, Biance. You gonna come with me?"

She nods her head while sucking her finger and drawing it out of her mouth with a loud 'pop'. I can't wait to sink my cock into her mouth so she can 'pop' it like that.

As I serve some more drinks, she waits at the end of the bar for me. There are a lot of gorgeous women in here tonight. Am I stupid just saving myself for one? I look over to Bianca, she smiles, and I know I'm making the right decision.

After twenty minutes, I shout over to Keaton, "I'm going for my break. Be back in …" I look over to Bianca, smile, and then say, "Back in half an hour." Keaton follows my eyes and smiles back at me.

"I'll cover for you. I'm sure there are a couple of ladies who want to see what I have to offer." He walks over towards the cocktail booth. "Right, ladies. Are you ready for some fun, Keaton style?"

They all shout "yeah" and he laughs, turning around to make some shots for the ladies.

Walking over to Bianca, I grab her hand and

pull her after me. This is going to be quick and hard. Taking her down the corridor past the toilets, I open the last door on the right. This is an office I use when Ainsley gets on my case about orders, taxes, and shit like that. She follows me in and I close the door and push her up against it.

Her breath catches. "So…" I say. "You like blow jobs then, huh?"

She nods.

"Tell me what you like?" I ask, while my hand is in her hair and pulling it so she has to look up at me.

"I love blow jobs and I want to give you one now." She starts to slide down the door, but I pull her up again.

"My turn first. It's my break and I'm hungry for your pussy."

She smiles and widens her legs for me. I was right; she opens them freely.

Slowly, I work my way down her body, kissing down her neck then her collarbone. I pull one of her breasts free of her red dress and her nipple stands erect, teasing me. I take it into my mouth and suck it, then I bite it.

"Oh my God, Hunter," she says, running her

hands though my hair and pushing me further down her body.

Kneading her breast, I kiss up her inner thigh. Using my other hand, I run it up and under her knickers. Actually, scratch that - her thong. She's wet and ready for me. I reluctantly leave her breast and use both hands to open her legs a little bit wider and then I use my fingers to open her lips. "Please… " she whispers.

I indulge her. I gently push my tongue along the inside of her lips until I reach her clit, then I start flicking and her body starts to tense under me.

"Relax," I say into her core. Her body relaxes a little bit. I grin. I run one of my fingers along her lips and then slide it inside her pussy.

"God, you're wet."

"I've been wet and ready since I took that drink off your cock," she says in a husky voice that goes straight to my cock.

Pulling my finger out, I thrust two of them back inside and start finger fucking her. She squelches she's that wet. I keep flicking her clit with my tongue and then when I start sucking it, she comes all over my fingers. That was a lot quicker than I thought it would be. I chuckle.

"Oh my God," she says breathlessly.

I suck on her pussy and swallow down her cum. It tastes good; a little salty, but good. When she's come down from her high, I slowly stand and kiss her so she can taste herself.

"My turn," she says, sliding down the wall again. This time I let her.

She reaches out and grabs my belt to undo my zip and my shorts then she reaches in and releases my cock.

I'm proud of my cock, just so you know. It's large, thick, and performs well.

"Hunter, the rumours about you are true. You are huge!"

"Stop talking and start sucking, babe. My break is nearly over."

She licks the end of my cock as there's some pre-cum from when she came. I love the sound of a woman orgasming; it really turns me on. She grabs the base of my cock and slowly swallows it all. She must have been practising with an ice pop or something, because, God, she can deep throat. Not many woman can do it right, but I can feel my cock slide past her tongue and down into her throat.

"God, Bianca. That feels so good." I push her head closer to my body. I hold her head in place, enjoying the sounds of her gulping and then I feel her head pull away so she can breathe. "You're like a real life porn star."

She smiles up at me and then resumes sucking and deep throating until I can't take anymore.

"I'm going to come, so if you don't want to swallow it, you better take it out of your mouth."

She looks up at me, smiles, and then opens her mouth wider. She takes the base of my cock and pushes it all in as far back as she can get it. My balls are touching her lips and she has her head tilted to take me all. I thrust slightly, knowing just that movement alone is going to make me jizz down her beautiful throat.

I pull back one last time and thrust in deep. She gulps and then I come deep in her throat. I hear her gulping again and I try to move backwards to let her breathe, but she digs her nails into my arse and keeps me in place until my cock has emptied everything it has down her throat. Then she pushes me away and I hear the big gasp of air she takes.

I lean down because I can see she's exhausted. "That was the best blow job ever," I say, kissing her lips.

When we stand, she wipes her mouth like I hoped she would. I smile. She adjusts herself and straightens herself out and then I give her a quick kiss on the lips and leave. "I'll see you later," I say, smacking her on the arse. She squeals and then giggles.

Keaton sees me coming back from my break and smiles at me. We high five each other and he says, "I'm off on my break now. I'm getting a bit of what you just got." He nods his head towards a little brunette at the end of the bar who is looking all doe-eyed at him.

I laugh and slap him on the shoulder. "Enjoy, but it won't be as good as my break."

He walks away, hooking his arm through the brunette's, going in the same direction I just came from.

The rest of the night is a huge success, and when it's time to slow things down, Skylar starts playing some slow songs. This is the moment when you see the once single people couple up ... at least for tonight.

I see Bianca looking at me and shake my head. I have to work. Even though the singles night is nearly over, we have a lot of cleaning up to do before we can leave. She throws back another couple of shots and I feel a little guilty, but I never said I was available for a relationship. She is purely 'fuck once' material.

Skylar finishes the music and then starts to pack everything away. I see a cute little redhead with a pixie cut, watching him. She looks shy, but he doesn't even notice her. I must mention it to him, because she looks like she's his type.

Ainsley is busy asking everyone to leave and Zac is doing what he does best - intimidating everyone to leave. It's very rare we get any trouble in here, Once they see him, they don't hang around long enough to cause trouble.

Bianca is hanging around at the bar, waiting for me to finish. Everyone else has left except the brunette Keaton was with earlier. I sidle up to Bianca. "Hey. I have to finish up here, but if you can wait half an hour I'll make it worth your while." I wink at her.

Her face lights up. "Okay. Can I have another Blow Job then?" she asks, looking coy.

I smile and make her one, making sure I put extra cream on it so I can see her wipe her mouth again.

She licks her lips as I hand it to her. She goes to grab it and I slide it back off her.

"Ah, ah, ah," I say. "No hands, babe. No hands."

I walk away, not able to watch her drink it

without her hands. There are only so many things my cock can take.

After cleaning up and sorting out the bar for tomorrow night, Keaton says to me, "Man, did you see her suck up her shot? I'd love that around my cock!"

I push him. "Fuck off. She's mine! Well, for tonight anyway." I laugh. I don't mind sharing. There's never enough women to go round.

After we're finished up, we all leave at the same time. They all go in their own directions, off to do who knows what, but I hook my arm through Bianca's and say, "How do we get to your place?"

I never bring them to my house. She is a random hook up and if she knows where I live then she might turn into a stalker and I don't need that.

———

When we get to hers and she opens the door, I push her in. I want to get hot and heavy, fuck her, and leave. Pushing her up against the wall, I start kissing her, pushing my tongue inside and pull her hair. She has her hands around my neck, pulling me closer.

"Hunter, we need to make it upstairs." She pulls away and I follow her as she runs up the stairs.

When we get into the bedroom, I push her down on the bed and start peeling her red dress off her. She has a fantastic figure and I can't wait to fuck her and watch her tits bounce up and down. They're so fake; I bet she can't even feel me touching them.

She lays on the bed naked and I take off my top and then my jeans. I'm commando, so I'm ready to go at any time. I kiss her body and take my time working my way down her. I can't wait too long; I need to be inside her. I touch her to make sure she's wet enough to take me.

"Bianca, I'm going to fuck you hard. I'm so horny and I need to come."

"Hunter, I want you so bad. Just fuck me."

I take a condom out of my back pocket, rip the packet, and cover my cock in plastic.

"Are you sure you're ready? This is going to be hard and fast."

She nods. I lean over her and kiss her again, letting my tongue slide into her mouth at the same time my cock pushes into her pussy.

"Oh my God." She moans into my mouth.

I hold still to let her get used to my size and then I ram myself fully in. She's wet and hot, but not very tight. Good job I'm big and can still feel her walls as she squeezes them around me. I don't really like the missionary position, it's quite boring, so I pull out and drag her down the bed. She smiles at me. "Hunter, what are you doing?"

"I'm changing it up, babe." I lift her up and she wraps her legs around my waist. I kiss her whilst moving her backwards until she's up against the wall. I slam into her and she climbs up my body and grabs the back of my head.

"Fuck, Hunter!"

"I know, babe. That's what I'm doing!" I keep slamming into her, and she keeps bearing down on me, meeting me stroke for stroke. She feels tighter in this position and she keeps squeezing me, sucking me in.

She starts to unravel around me. "Hunter... oh my God. I'm going to come." She squeezes me tight for the last time and then I push in as far as I can go. "Aargh!"

I lean in and rest my head against hers; we're both breathing heavily.

When I feel my heart rate starting to get back to normal, I slowly pull out of her and move her legs so that she's standing on the floor. "Can you stand on your own?"

"I... I think so." She takes the weight herself and then giggles. "I feel like Bambi."

I laugh. Taking a step back, I take the condom off and tie a knot in it. Looking around for a bathroom, she points to a door in the corner. Going inside, I throw it in the bin. I lean on the counter and look into the mirror. Sweat is pouring down my face, but I still look good.

When I walk back into the bedroom, she's in bed with the duvet folded back for me to get in too. Fuck. This is when it gets awkward. Walking over to my clothes, I start to put my jeans back on.

"Where are you going?" she asks pitifully.

"I'm not staying. I have to get home. I have some stuff to do before I go to sleep. I had a great time. Thanks, Bianca." I walk over, and leaning over her, I kiss her deep and hard. "See you again," I say, and walk out of the bedroom and her house.

I know I'm a bastard, but all she was is someone I hooked up with. I never asked for anything more and I never insinuated anything more.

Walking home, it's a nice night; warm and the moon is shining with not a cloud in the sky, guiding me home.

Walking along the promenade, I see a couple

making out in the deck chairs. I know it sounds impossible, but believe me, it's quite fun.

I feel like a stalker, but the woman isn't making nice noises. It sounds like he's forcing her to kiss him. I sit in one of the deck chairs just on the other side of a small wall. They can't hear me.

"Get off me," I hear her mumble as he grinds his mouth over hers.

"You know you want me to, Scarlett. You've been teasing me for long enough. Come on, baby… please," the guy says.

I can't listen to anymore. He needs to respect that when a woman says no, she means no. Even though I'm a player, I'd never force a woman to let me fuck her. I don't need to.

Standing I walk around to the other side of the wall and when I am in front of them I say, "Scarlett, are you okay?"

They both look at me. She nods.

He says, "Who the fuck are you? How do you know my girlfriend?"

He lets her go and starts to stand up, but she grabs his arm. "Finn, leave it alone. I don't know him."

He shrugs out of her grasp.

"She doesn't know who I am, but she doesn't

want you to push her either." I stand tall in front of him. He is a good few inches shorter than me and much, much leaner.

"Why do you think you can stick your nose in my business?" He stands on his toes so he can shout into my face.

I push him away slightly. "I don't know your girlfriend, but she said she didn't want to do whatever you were trying to make her do. Leave her alone."

She grabs his arm. "Come on, Finn. Leave it." She steps back into the beam of light from the street light behind the wall and I see her fully for the first time.

She is stunning. I catch my breath. Wow. I've seen a lot of extremely beautiful women in my time, but she makes them all pale into the background. The moonlight is shining on her beautiful honey-coloured hair like a halo, and she has curves in all the right places. She looks at me, smiles, and then looks away. She likes what she sees too.

After what happened to me at Uni I would never take another man's woman. I reach out and touch her to ask if she's happy to stay with him and I feel something I've never felt before. A shock runs through my body like I've met my other half, the missing part of me, the part that will make me whole. I shake my head and take my hand off her.

"Erm... Scarlett, are you going to be okay here?"

She jumps back slightly and just stares at me. I wonder if she felt it too? She looks shocked. "Erm... yeah. I'll be fine. Thank you." She smiles at me again.

I turn and walk away. It's really the last thing I want to do. I just want to knock him out and run away with her. I don't have these feelings; I must be drunk, although I know I haven't had many drinks tonight.

I hear Finn shout, "Fuck off, you nosy bastard. Come on, Scarlett. We can finish this at home."

I don't turn back around because it's really none of my business.

While walking through Royal Terrace Gardens - which used to be called Rock Walk when I was younger - to get home, I can't stop thinking about Scarlett and how I reacted to her touch. Stopping halfway up the steep steps, I turn and watch them walk away from the gardens towards the old harbour. She looks like she is putting up a bit of fight, but it's none of my business. I only turn and carry on up the hill when I can't see her anymore.

Taking the lift, which brings me straight into my penthouse apartment, I do what I always do when I get home from work. I go straight through the lounge and out onto my wraparound balcony. I just love looking at the bay at night. It's pitch black, but all the fairy lights brighten up the sky with their multicolours twinkling along the bay.

I breathe in the sea air and wonder why I ever left this town. I think I was getting smothered by the whole tourist thing going on, but since I've been back, I realise how beautiful my hometown is. After a few minutes, I walk back inside and go to bed. Fucking Bianca has worn me out.

PROLOGUE

How did I end up here? My body stinks from not having a wash in about two weeks. There's never any hot water for the showers and I don't even remember the last time I ate.

I hear the guy on top of me grunt as he finally has his orgasm. Thank god! There are only so many times I can count the ceiling tiles in this dank, dark and seedy room.

He rolls off me and I quickly get up and run to the bathroom, to wash away all signs of him.

Men only ever think of themselves and they are

incredibly selfish when it comes to shagging. They use my body like a vessel to dump their cum into and then they leave. That's the part I love the most ... the moment when they leave. This is what my life has become. I don't think back to better times when I felt safe, when I felt loved.

I open the door from the bathroom and see Barry on the bed, looking down at his hands. He does this every time, and I know what's coming next. *The guilt trip!* For him not me that's for sure.

He looks up when he hears me approaching. "I'm so sorry Whiskey, I shouldn't keep doing this. My wife would leave me if she knew I was having sex with you ... Regular sex with you. Why can't I stay away from you? How did you get under my skin?"

I tune out. He says this every week, it's getting really old. "Maybe you should go to your wife then, buy her some flowers or take her out for dinner tonight. Show her how much you love her."

I'm not upset. I'm not jealous, I'd have to have feelings to be jealous. It just seems to make him feel so much better for cheating on his wife when I send him away and tell him how to treat her nice.

"You're such a good girl Whiskey," he says standing up and tightening his belt. "I was lucky when I met you." He walks towards me and I think he is going to hug me, but he stops short of doing just that.

"So, goodbye then Barry" I say, as I do every week. He smiles and walks towards the door. "Thanks for being a great sport. I appreciate it and I *will* take my wife out tonight." Watching him grab the door handle I see him turn at the last minute. "Whiskey, I've left your money on the side. Same time next week then?"

I nod. His guilt trip didn't last long. He closes the door and when I have heard him retreating down the corridor, I lay on the bed and sob. I cry for how my life has ended up this way. I cry for everything I've lost ... my family ... my friends ... my hope ... but most of all I cry for losing my dignity.

———

1

"Get back in here, Polly!" I hear my dad shouting behind me as I run out of the house, down the path and off down the road. Who calls their little girl Polly anyway? I hate my name and it has been the cause of a lot of our arguments over the years.

"Why did you have to call me fucking Polly?" I scream at him, but he can't hear me as the wind carries my angry cries off and up into the sky.

My full name is Polly Penelope Parker! I mean how bad is that. I get teased about my name all the time – 'Pretty Polly', 'Polly lost her perch.' For fucks sake, what were my parents thinking of – not me that's for sure!

It drives me insane. My dad is a sergeant major type too, which makes it all so much worse. He never stops shouting at me. I can never do anything right in his eyes. I just need to get out of the house today, he was screaming at me about my school report. It wasn't that bad, but dad expects perfection and unfortunately, that is not my style.

I dress weirdly because I don't want people to talk to me, I'm quite brainy but I don't make any effort in class. I don't want the teachers to notice me and bring me to the attention of the other students. So basically, I sit at the back of each class only half listening and then I sneak out and sneak into the next class. Sometimes I feel like I am gliding along on the periphery of my existence.

Life is dull, boring and I can't keep doing this. Something will snap and I don't want to think about the aftermath THAT will cause. I keep walking ... I don't know where I am going ... I just need to get out of here.

Luckily, I had planned for this day. Not knowing when it would come, but wanting to be ready for it, I had stashed my rucksack in a black plastic bin bag, at the end of the garden under the big lavender bush we have. It is so big that thankfully nothing gets wet underneath it. I left my bag there about two months ago. Just ... In ... Case ... As I walk down the street I lean over the wall, grapple around under the bush trying to feel my bag. I lay my hand on it, thankfully, so I pull it out and hoist it on my back. It's not wet, thank god.

I keep walking ... I don't know where I am going ... I just need to get out of here.

Moving as fast as I can without drawing attention to myself I can't hear Dad calling after me anymore. I'm in the town centre before I know it and, being a Saturday, it's really busy. I lose myself in the crowd. Even if Dad followed me, which I very much doubt he would, then it would be hard to find me amongst the big crowds..

I continue power walking, not wanting to slow my pace ... not wanting to get caught. I decide I know where I'm heading ... to the train station ... Destination unknown!

The lights of the station are up ahead and I know I'm nearly home and dry. My heart is racing, both from the exercise and from the excitement of leaving home. When I walk through the entrance I stop to breathe for the first time since I left home. I bend over and rest my hands on my knees and just breathe. I was never good at running at school. Mr. Peters, my PE teacher, would be proud of me I made it here in double quick time.

The station is packed and I go straight up to the ticket office. It takes five minutes before I'm served and during that time my heart is beating so hard I can hear it in my ears. I keep looking around making sure Dad didn't follow me. Already I know he won't think I've come this far from home having never ventured this far from home before so I know he won't look for me here. The consequence of doing so is just too great. He would shout at me and make me cry and these days I think he is only one beat off hitting me.

It's eventually my turn and I step forward. "How can I help you today miss?" The old man behind the counter asks.

"Good," I say looking around me, not hearing what he asked me.

"Are you ok? Do you need help?"

I stutter, "Erm ... Erm no I'm fine thanks. What's the next train that leaves this station? When is it leaving and where is it going?"

He looks at me and then down at his screen. To me it feels like he is taking forever to find a train. I start moving from foot to foot, and I realise it looks like I need the toilet or something. My nerves are kicking in now the adrenaline is dissipating.

"Well miss, the next train to leave is going to Kings Cross Station in ten minutes and it's eighteen pounds and fifty-two pence."

I smile, Kings Cross ... that's in London. Do I want to go to London? Will I be able to survive London? Well, if I am going to go to anywhere in the country then London is as good a place as any. I can disappear and no one will be able to find me. It might even be the best place to go.

"Perfect, I'll take it," I say as I hunt through my bag looking for my purse.

"Do you want a return ticket?"

"No freaking way, I am never coming back here again." I say adamantly. Smiling I hand over twenty pounds and wait patiently for my ticket and my change.

"There you go love, platform four and you've got six minutes. Enjoy the capital."

Saying thank you I pick up my ticket and put the change in my pocket, it will come in handy on the four hour train journey. The journey which will be the start of my new life. Away from here, away from HIM.

———

2

It's been six months since I arrived at Kings Cross Station, with only my rucksack to keep me company. My life has changed so much since then. I have a great job in marketing, a fantastic apartment looking over the skyline of London City and a fantastic man that I love!

Do you really believe that bullshit right there? Life doesn't happen like that – well not for me anyway. Life is shit! That's all I can say. I didn't expect to arrive in London and land on my feet, but then again I didn't really have any type of plan when I jumped on the train that day.

As soon as I stepped off the train, I went to a hostel that I had seen advertised in Kings Cross Station Information Centre and asked if they had any room. My luck must have been in as they only had two beds left for the night.

Before I left the train station I had bought some food and as I went to my room I started thinking about my next step. When I walked in I noticed there were eight beds – eight beds! I'm an only child, so I'm not used to sharing my room! I took one of the spare ones and settled in for the rest of the day and night. Bearing in mind that I am only sixteen, well nearly seventeen, and have never been away from home, not even for a sleepover at a friends, I was really scared. My dad never let me go to my friends houses, he wanted to control me in everything I did. I shook my head to get those thoughts out of my mind. Google was my friend and I started looking for jobs and bedsits.

I had saved money from birthdays and Christmases for years saving nearly one thousand pounds which I had stashed in my rucksack. I don't intend to squander any of it. I was so tired that I fell asleep straight away that first night, but was woken up later in the middle of the night by my 'roommates' coming home at all hours.

I just turned over in the bed and ignored them. I had watched enough movies to make sure my purse was tucked down my pyjama bottoms so no one could steal it from me.

I woke up before everyone else the following morning and I had snuck out of the room. I made sure I booked another night and went off looking for work. I wasn't going to waste another moment – I need to find work to survive.

My innocence lead me to believe that everyone would be looking for people to work for them, cheap labour, but I was so wrong. Approaching about twenty five different places before lunch was tiring and disheartening because not one of them showed any interested. I stopped to have some lunch in a greasy spoon near Kings Cross and was surprised when I heard them moaning about how busy they were and how they needed help.

Not thinking twice I went up to them and offered my services. The guy looked me up and down, told me I was too young and turned back to getting stressed.

When I looked around there were lots of customers and they were all moaning about something. Without thinking about what I was doing I started clearing the tables, wiped them down and took orders from the customers who looked to me like they were going to leave. After that, they couldn't turn me down. I passed my initiation into 'Silver Spoon' a little café down one of the side streets near Kings Cross.

Silver Spoon was like a second home to me, working about thirty hours a week and then I would go home to the hostel at night. It was perfect except for a couple of the other girls in the room were loud, confident and had a drink or drug problem. Obviously, I didn't drink or do drugs, I was just too young for that.

When I had been at Silver Spoon for about six months, I knew that I needed to find somewhere else to live, but the wages I get from them is just too small for most of the apartments for rent.

"Jane! JANE! Are you not listening to me? Table three needs to be cleared." My boss, Dan, shouts across the café. Shaking my head to clear the thoughts of finding somewhere to live. I smile at him calling me Jane. Yes of course I changed my name, I didn't want anything to lead Dad to find me. However, when they asked me what it was, I couldn't think quick enough to give myself a really cool name. Jane just slipped from my lips. Jane – as in Jane Doe.

"Sorry Dan, just on that now." He works me like a Trojan and pays me like a slave, but he is a really nice guy who would do anything for me. He is always trying to find out more about me. Where I come from, what I am doing in London, but I never give in and tell him. He knows I'm young, but not exactly how young I am. He asks about my family but I always say that I don't have a family anymore.

Today is really busy, so when my shift is over I take a chance and ask him, "Dan, any chance of a few more hours? I could really do with the money, I need to find somewhere safe to live."

"Jane, I'm really sorry, you know I'd do anything to help you, but I can't stretch to any more hours."

"No problem, I'll have to go and find a second job because I really need to get some more money." I say wistfully as I walk over and clear the tables, ready to close up for the day.

Drifting back to the hostel after work, I'm deep in thought. Laying on my bed I start to cry. Was this really the right thing to do? Should I have just put up with my horrendous life back home with dad? At this moment in time, it feels like I should have stayed and put up with his dictatorship because I don't think I'm cut out for this ... for London.

"Are you ok Jane?" I hear someone who is kneeling at the side of my bed. It's Tilda. She was living here before me. She is gorgeous and is out every night in one designer outfit or another. I don't know why she stays here if she can afford those types of dresses.

Rolling over to face her I put a small smile on my face. She is one of the nicer girls that stay in this room, some of them are absolutely awful to me. Tilda has always been nice.

"I just don't know how to keep doing this. Maybe I should have stayed back home, this is really hard."

"What's hard hun? You arrived and almost straight away you got a job, most of us struggled for such a long time to get any work."

"I know, but I need more money. I can't stay here forever."

"You can stay as long as you want Jane, I've been here for two years. I'm saving up my money so that I can move into a fabulous apartment. Staying here helps me to save, because it's cheap, so much cheaper than a bedsit."

"I can't understand why you don't just leave here, you always look so glamorous, that I wonder why you are even here."

"I'll tell you my story another day. Look, what time do you finish work tomorrow? If you want we can meet up and go for a drink and talk. I'd like to spend some tie with you, we're roommates we need to know each other."

I don't want to tell her that I am only seventeen and can't legally drink. It was my birthday two months ago but I didn't tell anyone. Knowing that if I put some make up on then I will get into a pub no trouble, so there is no need to tell her I'm underage.

"I finish at four o'clock tomorrow."

"Great I'll meet you at the Nag's Head in Kings Cross, it's only around the corner from the Silver Spoon, we can have a really good talk then. I'm off to work now so I'll see you tomorrow. Keep smiling Jane, you have a gorgeous smile." She leans over and kisses me on the forehead and then she is gone. Her action makes me tear us. My mum used to kiss my forehead and thinking of her always makes me cry. We had a happy family until the day she died suddenly. Dad was devastated and that's when he started changing. He no longer showed me any emotion. He shut me out the day she died ad I lost two parents that day.

Laying on my bed I think about Tilda. It makes me think about her story, where did she come from? I wonder what kind of work does she do to dress like that every night, and I wonder what she wants to talk to me about.

After a full day at work I'm exhausted and fall asleep easily, only to be woken three or four times during the night, as usual, when the rest of the girls come home.

———

3

Work can't finish any quicker for me. I am dying to meet Tilda and see what she has to offer me. I really need some work and at this stage I will do anything to try and make something of myself.

"Jane, where are you? I know you're not in this café right now. Earth to Jane!" Dan chuckles behind me.

"Sorry Dan, I was miles away."

"It's ok, I thought you might have found yourself a fella or something."

"No chance of that," I laugh. "I don't go anywhere except here and the hostel."

"Really? You should get out more Jane, you're a very pretty girl."

"Thanks," I blush. "I just want to concentrate

on work and get enough money to do something with my life."

"You have great drive and enthusiasm Jane. The way you forced my hand at giving you a job, I'm sure you will be able to achieve whatever you set your heart on."

"Thanks Dan." I do something totally unchar- acteristic and I go over and hug him. He pauses for a moment before he wraps his arms around me and hugs me back. I start to whimper because this man has shown me more love in the last six months than my dad ever did. I bet he hasn't even bothered to look for me. He probably thinks that I will stroll back into the house one day, well that isn't going to happen!

We awkwardly pull apart. "Don't you ever tell the other staff I hugged you, they don't deserve hugs." He says smiling at me before he walks away.

"Don't worry, the secret of your soft side will be safe with me." I shout after him.

I hear him laugh, a real belly laugh. It's conta- gious and it puts a smile on my face.

When my shift is over, I say goodbye to Dan and walk over to the Nag's Head. Tilda is already waiting for me, thank god. I'm worried walking in that they might ask me for ID, but I had nothing to worry about, they didn't even blink an eye at me.

"Hey Jane, come sit down, I got you a drink." She points to a glass with orange liquid in it.

"What's THAT?" I ask picking it up and smelling it.

"Vodka and red bull. It will give you the buzz, loosen you up a little, you always look like you have the whole word on your shoulders."

"Oh, erm, I don't really drink Tilda." "What? Who in their right mind doesn't drink as a teenager?" She looks at me like she is seeing me for the first time. "How old are you?"

This is it. This is the moment that I have been waiting for. I take a deep breath, "Eighteen. I'll be Nineteen in May." Well my life did start again when I got here six months ago, so that is now my new birthday.

"Ok, good, because I thought for a minute there you were underage." She laughs. I smile and giggle too, but for different reasons.

We talk for about half an hour about what I'm doing in London and what my goals are. She stands and goes to the bar to get another vodka red bull for both of us. I can feel it working already, I feel hot but I can feel the ice cold of the drink running through my veins. My tongue is feeling looser and my body is starting to relax.

"So, I know you are looking for more work and wondered if you would be interested in what I do. We are looking for someone who looks young, but has some savvy about her. I thought of you straight away. You kind of fit that description."

I take a sip and savour the taste in my mouth. She is watching me, waiting for my reaction. I swallow with a big gulp.

"W ... What is it you do? I know you are always dressed in gorgeous clothes and I can't ever imagine being able to afford them."

She smiles and smooth's her dress down her exquisite body. "It has taken a while to be able to afford these dresses, but you would be able to as well if you decided to work with us."

"OK. Tell me more. I'm intrigued."

She takes a sip of her drink, then a big breath. "I belong to an agency called Kings X Companions."

I put my glass down. "Go on!" I say hanging on to her every word.

"I know it sounds like we are dirty whores, but believe you me, we are far from that. We escort business men to functions. Being based in Kings

Cross is great because we can meet them from the train ready to go wherever they want us to."

Not knowing what to say, I take another sip of my drink, letting it flow through my veins and relax me, because all of a sudden I feel very uptight.

She takes a sip of her drink, carefully watching my face, knowing I won't interrupt she carries on. "We meet them wherever we are told to meet them. We always get a description of them, so we know who we are looking for and they have a description of us too. We spend the evening with them, usually we go for dinner or they take us to an event. Most of these men just want some company while in on business. We also accompany businessmen who live in London when they need to go to functions. We become their plus one!"

"So, you get a free dinner and you get paid for keeping them company for a few hours a night?" "Yes exactly! Most of the men I have met are really good fun and there are some good looking ones too, which always makes it easier."

"Let me get my head around this. You meet guys. You have dinner, dance a little and then you go home. Is that right? Or do you HAVE to have sex with them too?" I blush at the thought of men paying to have sex with Tilda. She's too beautiful for that.

Her head snaps up to look at me. "I'm not a prostitute Jane!" She is getting angry, but one look at my face and she realises that I wasn't calling her one. I was just curious.

"I didn't mean it like that Tilda, I just don't see how a man would pay a lot of money and not expect sex at the end of the night. That's my assumption from living here for the last six months."

She laughs. "Well in the normal run of things, yes men do expect you to sleep with them, but with Kings X Companions, that isn't the case."

"Well if that's the case then I'd be very interested."

"However," she says, "a man 'might' proposition you and it's up to you whether you sleep with him or not. The company doesn't offer it as a service, however, we are allowed to organise that between ourselves."

"But ... but doesn't THAT make you a prostitute?"

"NO! We are high class escorts, that's totally different. A prostitute is someone who sells sex on the corner of the street for twenty, thirty or forty pounds." "So how much do you make for sleeping with someone?" I'm really confused. I don't think I understand the difference.

"It depends on the guy really. If he wants sex with you then he will make an offer, but we never accept less than one hundred and fifty an hour. If they want anything kinky, and we're happy to do it, then we charge more. They might negotiate on a 'full night' where you stay over with them. That figure is up to you, but if it is something you are interested in then I'll help you with that."

"I think I need a drink." I say looking down at my, now empty, glass. I stand and walk to the bar, I know she is staring at me, I can feel her eyes boring into my back.

"Can I have a Whiskey please? Straight up and on the rocks." My dad used to order that and I feel like I need one right now. I used to watch him throw the whiskey into himself and then he would change again. This time he would be stronger, angrier and more determined to make my life hell!

The barman pours one for me and I knock it straight back. It burns my throat, but it's the pain I need. "Can I have another one please and also a vodka red bull? Thank you."

He looks at me and I think he is going to ask for

ID, my heart is racing and I make a mental note to get some fake ID. He smiles at me then goes off to pour two more drinks. After I have paid for them I take them back over to Tilda and sit down. "You're pale, are you ok Jane?" She asks.

"I'm just trying to get my head around the whole companion business. I was really excited until you got to the sex part."

She laughs. "Don't get hung up on the sex, Jane. If you don't want to have sex with the guy, then you don't have to. Just like if you are on a date with someone. I'm sure you've been out since you've been here, had a guy approach you and you have thought about having sex with him."

I take a quick gulp of my drink, my last sexual encounter didn't go well at all. I had a boyfriend back home and we had 'experimented' and then I met a guy here a couple of months ago on a work night out. I went back to his place and had sex with him, it wasn't good sex and when he was asleep I crept out of his room and went back to the hostel.

"Oh ... my ... god you're not a virgin are you?" She says sitting forward in her seat so she is closer to me.

"No I am not!" I say taking another sip of my whiskey.

"That's good you had me worried there for a bit. This is no different to going on a date." She continues. "You spend the evening with a mannerly man, who has been fully vetted and he wines and dines you then you can either say goodbye or stay longer and earn more money."

"Well, when you put it like that it's not too bad then. How much do you get for doing the companion part?" "We usually get seventy five pounds an hour." I splutter and nearly choke on my drink "WHAT? HOW MUCH?"

"Shh, stop shouting Jane, you don't want everyone to know. You might start at fifty pounds an hour when you start but after a few months, if you are getting recommendations, then you will move up to seventy five pounds an hour."

I sit there with my mouth open, counting on my fingers. "So, on average you work for maybe six hours at seventy five pounds, that's ... four hundred and fifty pounds!" I take another sip of my drink! I think I need it.

"Yes that's about it! It's fun, you get to go to so many nice restaurants, party venues and just have fun. Occasionally, you will go with a really boring guy but it's still worth it for the money alone."

"Can I think about it Tilda? I like the idea of

the money, but not sure about the sex part of it. Don't get me wrong, I'm not a virgin. I just don't know how I feel about people paying to have sex with me. In my eyes it's still prostitution, but I don't say as much to Tilda.

"Of course you can, but the reason this has cropped up now is that we have a customer who is in his early twenties, he has his own gaming company. He asked for a younger girl so you would be absolutely perfect. I said to the boss lady, Carla, that I would let her know tomorrow. Is that enough time to think about it Jane?" "Yeah I suppose." I need the money and it's easy money to be honest, but what if he asks to have sex with me? I just don't know how I feel about that.

"OK, in the meantime let me show you some of the venues I've been to and some photos of the guys I've met just to try and help your decision."

We sit there for another couple of hours, while she shows me, on her phone, all the photos of her dates and the places that they visited. It all looks fabulous, very much what my dreams are made of. Living the high life and getting paid for it.

"Tilda, can I ask you something?" She nods. "Are you sure I would fit in? You are all so beautiful and I'm just a plain Jane!"

"No you're not. You ARE beautiful, you just can't see it yourself."

"Tilda, look at you – you're gorgeous; blonde curly hair, super sexy figure and you dress to impress."

"I didn't start this way Jane, look." She takes her purse out of her bag and shows me a picture of her when she first arrived in London. She looks a bit like me. Nondescript! I gasp.

"Wow, you WERE like me!"

"Yes, I was. Now YOU can be like me. You already know I have a load of dresses which you can borrow. If you decide to do this and want your own dresses then I can take you out and buy you some clothes. You can pay me back when you get enough money, no rush. I'll also organise a make up session so that you can learn how to apply makeup to make the most of your features. Lingerie is really important, Jane, I can help you with that too."

"Really? You would do that for me?" I can feel my eyes filling with tears, she is being so kind and helpful.

"Yes, you look as vulnerable as I was when I first moved here. Someone took me under their wing and I have always been grateful for that."

"Why do you still live in the hostel then Tilda?

Surely you have enough money to move out and get somewhere swanky."

"Yeah I do, but I quite like living with you guys. You keep me stable and grounded. It reminds me of where I came from. I think I would be lonely if I lived on my own. Does that sound sad?"

"No, I feel the same way."

We laugh and get another drink. She's not at work today so we go back to the hostel where she lends me a dress and does my make up. I feel like a little girl playing dress up and when I look in the mirror I can feel the tears starting to build up. I never had this with anyone before. Dad wouldn't allow it and Mum died too early, I was only five when she died. Dad didn't know about my boyfriend and it was hard to keep up the secrecy.

I don't have to worry about that now, I have Tilda and I can't believe everything she is doing for me. "Don't you like it? You look fucking sexy Jane! No plain Jane tonight!" "I ... I ... love it! I look so different. What are we going to do tonight?" "We are going out! We've got our glad rags on and we are going to p-a-r-t-y!" She giggles. "Come on let's go and show this town what having a good time is all about!"

She takes me to a couple of local pubs and then

we go to Madame JoJo's in Soho, I've heard a lot about it, but I've never been there. I've not really been out of the Kings Cross district since I've been in London. I was worried about venturing too far and getting lost to be honest. Madame JoJo's is a dancing club and there are girls on the stage dancing burlesque and it is mesmerizing.

I'm having a great night and Tilda is such good company, I really like her. Our dresses and appearance get us in on the VIP list, I can't believe it.

"This is an amazing night, Tilda. Thank you for bringing me and helping me."

"You're welcome Jane, here's to the future."

We clink our glasses and toast to the future. We keep dancing and being hit on by good looking men until we get home at four in the morning and roll into bed.

4

Obviously, I took the job. I mean come on, who wouldn't want fancy dresses, high class restaurants and celebrity parties at least three times a week and get paid to do it all!

Exactly!

I stayed working for Dan in the Silver Spoon for as long as I could, but I had to give that up about twelve months later. I couldn't do the late nights and early mornings. I had cut my hours down and then finally handed my notice in and spent my life working for Kings X Companions. When I first started working with them, they told me my name wasn't sexy enough and wanted me to pick a new one! Tilda jumped in and said 'Whiskey', I looked at her and she whispered, "You always drink Whiskey, so why not?" I nodded and so Whiskey was born.

I had quickly moved from new girl to most recommended and, therefore, my hourly rate increased too. I was earning a fortune!

Yes, I slept with some of the men, but not all of them.

Whiskey

It didn't feel wrong, because I didn't have sex with the ones who didn't attract me. That's ok isn't it? Like Tilda told me at the start, it's just like going on a night out and having a one night stand, except I get paid for it!

Tilda and I have talked about getting our own place together, but we are still living in the hostel.

We have high dreams and want our first place to be spectacular, we don't want to settle for anything mediocre, regardless of how long it takes.

Madame JoJo's had enthralled me when we had gone there. The women there were so sexy and sensual that I knew I wanted to be like them. It was after going on my first job with the young guy Tilda told me about, that I came to the decision that because of my lack of experience I wasn't sensual enough. I felt clumsy and unsexy around him, so after doing some research I found they were holding burlesque lessons at Madame JoJo's. I jumped at the chance to learn some sensual moves which I could use on my dates.

I found my niche in life:- being a companion, dancing and just having fun. Now THIS is living the dream!

There are a few customers who always request me when they are here in London. I look forward to them coming back, it's like meeting an old friend again, only with greater rewards.

Tonight I am meeting a new customer. I always get a thrill when I get given the details and I try to research them if I can. Tilda is watching me get ready to meet Sawyer Callahan, the CEO for the Callahan group of Nightclubs. He has exclusive nightclubs all over the world and he is based out of New York. He is coming to London to scope out possible nightclubs to buy, renovate and recreate his signature style.

He is attending a charity function tonight in London at The Ivy. I've been there a couple of times and I've really enjoyed it. This time though it is in a private function and there will be lots of business people there rather than an intimate dinner for two. It's easier having dinner in a group, especially if my date is boring. I saw some pictures of him and he is really handsome! Like seriously handsome. I'd find it hard to turn down sex with him if he offers.

Tonight I am wearing a new dress which I haven't worn before. It is different shades of turquoise, starting at the bustier with a dark turquoise and flowing all the way down to the floor to a very pale turquoise. It makes me feel like a mermaid and there is a really sexy split up my left leg, stopping at my mid thigh. Stunning, if I do say so myself!

My hair has been curled by Tilda and then she carefully applied my make up. I finish it off with a turquoise choker that I bought especially to go with the dress. "Wow Whiskey, you look amazing! He is not going to know what has hit him when he meets you."

When I look in the mirror, I gasp. The person looking back at me is beautiful. I can't believe I look so good. I hope he is good company, I feel like tonight will be a good night. I'm quite nervous, as apart from his nightclubs, there is not much information about him. "Where are you meeting him?" Tilda asks. We always make a note of who we are meeting and where, just in case something goes wrong.

"His train is coming in to Paddington from the airport in about half an hour, so I'm going to meet him there. I have a plaque with his name on it." I show her the professional sign I had made for him.

"Great, do you want me to come with you and hide, or will you be ok?"

"I'll be fine. Anyway, don't you need to be in Piccadilly Circus to meet Drake?" Drake is her customer for the night. "Yeah I do, but I wanted to help you if you needed it." I laugh, "Tilda I'm fine, I'll see you tomorrow, hopefully." She laughs. "Yeah see you tomorrow." We hug and I leave to make my way over to Paddington. It is buzzing at this time of night. I don't think it is possible to go into Kings Cross Station and for it be empty, the hustle and bustle all starts here. I take a taxi to Paddington and it only takes about ten minutes.

After the taxi has dropped me off I check the arrivals board and see that his train is due in about ten minutes. Making my way to the platform I feel a surge of excitement rush through me. I stand at the end waiting for him with my sign.

Even with the long coat I have on, I know that I still stand out. I look too glamorous amongst all the commuters, the business people and the students.

His train pulls in and I get that fluttering feeling in my stomach, I'm excited to meet him. It's always nice to meet someone new, but there is something about his picture that makes me extra excited.

I see him before he sees me. He is gorgeous, his picture doesn't do him any justice whatsoever. I can actually feel myself blush when he looks up at me and smiles.

"Hi. Whiskey isn't it?" He says taking me into a hug. "Thanks for meeting me." He kisses me on both cheeks. I blush. He grabs my arm with one hand and carries his suitcase with the other. Outside he opens the door to a waiting taxi and I climb in, after he climbs in next to me, he leans forward and says to the driver "Hotel Intercontinental on Park Lane please."

"Right sir."

I have never been to the Intercontinental before and I've heard so much about it.

Sawyer turns to face me. He looks at me for a while and says, "You are much prettier than in your picture." He holds out his hand for me to shake.

"So are you." I say smiling at him as I reach out with my hand. Before I have the chance to shake his hand, he pulls it up to his mouth and kisses it, not breaking eye contact with me.

"Do you know where we are going tonight, Whiskey?"

"I believe we are going to The Ivy." His eyes never leave mine. He has me mesmerised.

"I think we are going to get on well. How did you get the name Whiskey?"

"Don't you think I was born with it?" I ask sassily.

He laughs, "Unless your parents were alcoholics then no, I don't think so." I try not to think about life back home, I shake my head trying to get rid of those thoughts.

Taking a deep breath I say, "Buy me a Whiskey later and I'll show you why." I wink at him. He smiles and then he takes my hand and interlocks his fingers with mine. I feel my whole body shake when he squeezes my hand.

I wouldn't normally be demonstrative with any of my customers unless it was in the bedroom, but clearly he feels he needs to have some contact for us to look like a couple or something.

He is quiet on the taxi journey, but he never once lets my fingers go. He leans back and rests his head on the back of the car seat and then he closes his eyes. This gives me a great opportunity to sit and really take a look at him and study him closely. He is a fine specimen of a man. There will be some very lucky lady out there if she gets to have him in her bed every night. I can just hope I get him for tonight. I shiver at the thought of it. "Are you cold?" He says, surprising me. He turns his head so that he can see me when he opens his amazing blue eyes.

I can't speak. I don't know how I am going to get through tonight, just looking at him makes me weak at the knees.

"I asked you a question. Are you cold?" He sounds upset.

"No, I'm not. I was just thinking about tonight."

He smiles at me and turns his head back to relax against the headrest.

After a couple more minutes the taxi pulls up at the very grand entrance to the Hotel Intercontinental. I can't help staring at the door leading inside, it is beautiful.

Sawyer pays the taxi, then climbs out holding his hand out for me to take to help me out. I take it and step out into the warm night. He doesn't let go of my hand and he almost drags me into the hotel.

At reception, after he checks in he is given a key to one of the penthouse suites. Of course he does. Where else would this gorgeous businessman stay?

"Do you want me to stay down here while you go and freshen up?" I ask not knowing what he wants me to do.

He looks at me as if I am stupid or something. "No, why would I want that? You are here for the night so why would I want you to stay downstairs while I go upstairs. That doesn't make sense." I suppose he has a point. He takes my hand again and pulls me so that I get in the lift with him, when the doors close he leans against the wall and just stares at me. He's making me feel uncomfortable, he hasn't even let go of my hand.

"Do I have something on my chin?" I ask with real attitude.

He smiles, "No!"

That's it, that's all he is going to give me. He is starting to really piss me off. He doesn't say very much does he?

When the lift opens, he pulls me out and into the suite. We both stop as we walk through the door. "This place never ceases to amaze me with it's beauty," he says closing the door behind me.

"Wow, Sawyer this place is amazing. It's so beautiful." I take a look around the suite. I'd never be able to afford something like this extravagant.

"Yes, yes it is," he says turning to face me. He takes my second hand and looks me in the eye. He is looking at me so intently that I think he is going to kiss me. I don't know how I feel about that. Usually when a customer kisses me, it's when we are in public and need to put on a front for the sake of business, it's never in private, that would be too intimate.

When he breaks eye contact with me I notice his suitcase is already here. I don't know how it arrived so quick, but he takes his suit out of his suit carrier and then goes into the bathroom to change.

I'm torn between having a look around and trying to sneak a peek at Sawyer changing his clothes. I decide that I would look like a stalker if I did that so I have a look out of the window looking at the view down below.

He comes out of the bathroom and I have to do a double take. If I thought he looked handsome in his business clothes, he looks stunning in his tuxedo. I take a deep breath and swallow hard, he is gorgeous.

"Are you ready to go?" He asks looking at my lips. I can't help but look at his, they look so succulent. "Let's go to the bar and have a drink first, it's going to be a long boring night, so we might as well make the most of it." He doesn't wait for my answer, and after grabbing my hand he turns and pulls me along with him to the waiting lift.

When we get to the lobby we go into the bar - The Lobby Lounge. It's beautiful. "What would you like to drink ... whiskey?" He smirks.

"Yes, please. Straight on the rocks please." His eyebrow lifts at one side, he thinks I am joking and don't really drink whiskey. Well, if that's the game he wants to play then I am all over that. I have drunk a lot of whiskey since that first one in the Nags Head with Tilda.

He places my drink on the table and I see that he got the same for himself. I lift my glass and raise a toast, "To a great night, Sawyer."

I smile and he raises his and repeats my toast. "To a great night, Whiskey."

I take a sip and I savour every drop of it. We keep our eye contact, not dropping it once.

"So, what do you think you are drinking?" He asks with a smile on his face.

I laugh, he shouldn't play this game with me. "Well, it's fruity and has a slight almond smell to it." I take another sip and close my eyes to try and break down the flavours in my mouth. When I open them he is staring at me, smiling.

"Well, what else can you tell me?" Ooh he's impatient.

"It has a hint of chocolate and orange, so it could be an Isle of Jura, but a distinguished palette would know it's a Chivas Regal." He smiles, watching my lips the whole time. "However, it's not just a normal Chivas, it's an old one." I take another smell and then a sip. "Now is it a twenty one year old one or the twenty five year old bottle, that is the question?"

His eyes leave my mouth and move directly to my eyes. "I'm impressed so far. See if you can pull it out the bag, Whiskey and if you can then I promise to buy you a bottle."

He's putting the pressure on me now. Those

bottles sell for nearly two hundred and fifty pounds each.

After another sip I close my eyes. It's very smooth and more refined so I think it is definitely the older one. "I believe this is the Chivas Regal twenty five year old scotch."

He smiles and his eyes sparkle. "I am extremely impressed Whiskey, you do live up to your name-sake. What else are you going to impress me with this evening?"

"Oh I don't know, maybe my wit and intelligence." I smile and giggle.

"Well your giggle impresses me already. I think tonight is going to be fun after all. I was worried that it would be boring, but I can see that it's already exceeded my expectations."

I blush, assuming he is meaning me. This man makes me weak at the knees.

"I'm just going to organise a car to take us to The Ivy so we can get this business thing over with and then we might go to a club and check out the competition."

"Sounds like a plan," I say demurely. He walks over to the bar and talks to the barman, he is there for quite a while and then comes back over with a smile on his face. "Come on then Whiskey, lets go and have some fun."

He holds out his hand to help me up, I take it. I like the connection we have when his skin touches mine. He lets go of my hand to take my arm and he manoeuvres me towards the front door and the waiting limousine. I always get excited when I am given a ride in a limo as it is such a luxury and I makes me feel like a child going to a big girls party.

Once we are both safely in, Sawyer closes the vanity screen and then he turns to me. "You are really beautiful and I want to kiss you. Is that allowed?"

It's a strange question, maybe he hasn't had a 'companion' before. I nod, "Yes it's allowed ... most things are allowed." I don't really want to get into the conversation about sex this early in the night, but it might make the night more fun if we both know what is going to happen at the end of the night.

"Hmm most things. I wonder if the things that I have in my mind that I want to do to you are allowed."

Now I know I am blushing. "You'll only find out if you ask me." I say breathing erratically. This discussion got serious really fast.

He smiles and very slowly he leans forwards, his lips getting closer to mine with every millimeter he moves, it seems like he takes an age. Eventually his lips touch mine, very softly and very gently and then the limo stops and the driver comes through the intercom "The Ivy, sir."

Sawyer groans. He looks at me, "This isn't over by a long shot. I've only just begun." He smiles and steps out of the limo, holding his hand out for me to take. When I stand out of the limo he says, "You look beautiful, I am a very lucky man tonight."

"Yes you are!" I say smiling at him. He chuckles and takes my arm and leads me into The Ivy.

We get shown to the function room in The Ivy. I've never been here before I've only ever been down in the restaurant, which is beautiful, but this is amazing. I can't stop looking around and taking it all in. Very art deco and there are so many beautiful women that I start to feel out of my depth.

When we get to our table, Sawyer pulls my chair out "Sit, Whiskey."

I do and he pushes my chair in, ever the gentleman.

The dinner is magnificent and I can't believe how much I have enjoyed myself with Sawyer; he is funny, has a lot to talk about and he is very gentlemanly.

After dinner we move around the room, Sawyer stopping to talk to people. I stand politely and then he puts his hand on my lower back and maneouvres me to the next person he wants to talk to. This happens for about half an hour and I've noticed his hand doesn't leave my back, even when he is standing talking to other businessmen.

I like the feel of it. I can feel the heat coming off his hand and warming me. We walk up to another couple. They all look the same;- older guy, younger woman who is extremely glamorous hanging off his arm. A little bit like us, I think sadly. The woman in front of us, can't keep her eyes off Sawyer, he hands down beats all the men in the room for good looks.

"So, Sawyer," the gentleman says. "Who is this gorgeous lady you are flaunting around tonight?"

Sawyer looks at me and smiles, his hand moves further around my waist and he pulls me in closer. "This is 46 Whiskey Whiskey, my date for the night." He leans over and kisses me on the cheek. That's when I feel something I have never felt before in my life. I've read about it, but have never experienced it myself. It feels like he's touched my skin with a bare wire charged with enough electricity to make me jump ten foot in the air. He pulls back quickly and I wonder whether he felt it too.

I blush ... He gasps ... He definitely felt something.

'S ... sorry, I need to excuse myself," I look at him and say. He nods and removes his hand from my waist.

After turning and walking away I hear the lady say, "She's not your usual type Sawyer."

I only hear part of his reply, "Thought I'd try something different ......"

I walk quickly to the bathrooms, I need some space. What the fuck just happened? Why did his kiss affect me so much? He's a customer ... he's a customer ... I need to keep repeating it to myself and remember I'm not on a real date. I think I forgot myself for a while.

I apply my lipstick and lean on the sink taking a deep breath when THAT woman comes into the toilet. She sees me and she smiles. Here it comes ... I just know she is going to say something bitchy.

"Hi, my name is Sasha," she says holding her hand out to shake mine. I extend mine and give her a tight gripped shake. "I'm Whiskey," I answer looking her over, replicating what she is doing to me.

"You're very lucky to get Sawyer, he is a real catch. He pays for all the extras as well." She watches my face as she slips in that she knows I am a companion.

"Did you really think no one knows he is paying for you tonight?" She laughs and it is a real whiny, bitchy laugh. "Darling, he always pays. He doesn't date the same woman twice. He must have gone through all the ladies at Mayfair Ladies and he's now moved on. Where is it you work?"

"Who says I work anywhere? Who says he is paying for this date?" I ask haughtily.

She laughs, like really laughs. "I'm sorry honey, but he always pays, everyone knows you are an escort! Don't let it put you off, you will be inundated with work after tonight. Everyone wants to have the girls that Sawyer has. You will be loaded by the end of the month!" She gives me one last look and then walks out of the bathroom laughing.

Standing there I feel hurt. I don't know why, but I pride myself in not behaving in a way that someone watching me would think that the man beside me is paying for me. I hate the thought of that, even though I do get paid. I take a few deep breaths, put a smile on my face and go out to find Sawyer.

As soon as I walk out the bathroom I feel someone grab my arm and drag me down the corridor. I start to panic, but the feeling of their hand calms me down, I know it's Sawyer. At the end of the corridor is a small doorway and he pulls me through it and pushes me up against the wall.

"Where were you? You've been gone a long time. Sasha came back and joined us a while ago." He's not angry, he's more concerned.

"I went to the bathroom, there's no law against that you know." Sasha's pissed me off and I can't hold back my tongue. I don't know why I am annoyed that he hires escorts all the time, it shouldn't matter to me, but it does.

He looks at me like I've upset him, then he smiles and moves closer to me. "You've got a little bit of fire in your belly, I like that. Did Sasha say something to you in the toilet?"

He reaches out and takes my chin in between his thumb and his index finger. "Tell me what she said?" He's growling at me.

"She didn't say anything," I say, looking down at the floor.

"Look at me when I'm talking to you!" He almost shouts in my face.

I look up into his eyes, I don't want him to see how much I am affected by him right now. "She didn't say anything."

"You're lying to me, Whiskey. I can tell. Let me guess what she said. She told you that I use escorts all the time. Am I right?"

I nod, as well as I can with his hands still on my face.

"Why does that bother you? Why does it bother me that it bothers you?"

"I ... I don't know. I know I'm a whore and nothing I ever do will change that, but to have someone call me out and accuse me to my face, that hurts."

"Look at me and not the floor!" I raise my eyes to meet his.

He leans forward and kisses me on the lips, urgently in between saying, "You .... Are ... Not ... A ...Whore!"

I'm stunned that he kissed me like that. "Sawyer, you and I both know that's not true. I am a whore. I let men take me out and then I charge them to sleep with me. That makes me a WHORE!." I feel like I want to cry. I have never felt like a whore, not until tonight and I don't like the feeling it gives me. I need to have a serious talk with Tilda tonight because I need to know how I can carry on with this job, thinking the way I do.

He stands back and takes a really good look at me. I feel disgusted, like he is looking to see how much of a whore I really am.

"Whiskey," he says taking my two hands in his. "You are a beautiful woman, men want to date you, where is the problem with that?"

"That's not what I mean – you know that."

"So are you going to change? Are you going to give up your job because of one woman who works in the same industry as you and is jealous because she is with Bill and not me? That's all it is Whiskey, jealousy. Now let's enjoy the rest of the evening. We can get out of here in a while and go to a nice club I want to look at."

"I'm sorry, you don't need some woman having a meltdown. I suppose that's why you never date and always hire someone."

"Exactly, I don't need this shit!" He takes my hand and drags me out of the room and back to the function room. He then puts his arm around my back and guides me around the room, talking to people as we go. Business as normal.

I feel stupid for being sensitive, but she made me realise what I truly am. I see her and Bill approaching Sawyer and I hold my breath.

She smiles at me and then I see her eyes linger on him longer than necessary. He's right, that's all she is – jealous!

"Are you ok Whiskey?" Bill drawls, smiling at me. "Yes, sorry I got talking in the bathroom." "Bill, Sasha, we are going to leave, we have another

business engagement this evening" Sawyer says, turning to smile at me.

"I'm sure you do," Sasha says under her breath, but loud enough for me to hear.

I feel Sawyer tense beside me, then he turns me to face him and kisses me in front of them. Now when I say kiss, I actually mean he devours me. I can feel it from the tips of my toes all the way to my lips. I am weak at the knees and he feels me crumble and pulls me closer to him.

When he pulls away I feel a big sense of loss and it's only when I look at Sasha I see that she is stood with her mouth open. "Come on babe, let's go. It was nice to see you both again." He says turning me around and putting his arm around me.

As we are walking out of The Ivy he says "Did you see her face?" Then he starts laughing.

"What's so funny? Do you want to share the joke?"

"I took her out for dinner ONCE, I never kissed her the whole night. I don't kiss anyone ... EVER!"

"But ... but you kissed me earlier."

"I know!" He leaves it at that and gets into a waiting taxi, making sure I get in before him. He doesn't let go of my hand for the whole journey, but he just looks straight ahead the whole way to our next destination.

When we pull over, I see we are at the Velvet Rooms. I know this as they were around the corner till it's lease ran out and the moved into new premises. I'm excited to go in here and have a big smile on my face.

"Come on, let's go inside and party," he says pulling me behind him.

"Yes, sir!" I say saluting with my spare hand. We manage to jump the queue, he must have connections. He takes me through to the VIP section and then he goes and orders me a drink – a whiskey. I smile at him as I take it.

We clink glasses and take a sip. I turn to look out at the club and he slides up next to me and wraps his arm around the bottom of my back and pulls me close. "I'm so glad I met you tonight."

"Me too," I say before I remember that this isn't a real date.

He kisses me on the cheek and again I feel the electricity shooting through me. He really does do things to my body that drive me insane.

After mingling for an hour he tells me that he wants to go back to the hotel. This is always the part of the evening I hate. Will he drop me off on the way? Will he invite me back? Will he want me to sleep with him? What about the money?

"Why are you worrying? What is going through your mind right now?"

I look him in the face and know that I will tell him exactly what is going through my mind because Sasha told me he never sees the same escort more than once. So if this is my one and only chance to fuck Sawyer, then I want to take it.

"I was wondering if you are going to fuck me tonight?"

He looks gob smacked! "That's not very nice language for a young woman, Whiskey. But seeing as you asked so nicely, it would be rude of me to say no!"

I feel myself release the breath I was holding. I smile and then look down at my lap. I don't know what to say now.

"Do you want me to fuck you Whiskey? How much do you want me to fuck you?"

Every time he says the word 'fuck' my pussy clenches. This is going to be enjoyable!

"I really want you to fuck me, hard." His eyes light up, he obviously enjoys it when I talk

dirty to him. I put that little bit of information to the back of my mind for use when we are on our own later on.

"Oh believe me, I am definitely going to do that." The taxi pulls up outside the hotel and after paying he drags me into the hotel. He stops at the bar on the way. It surprises me, I thought he wanted to go straight upstairs. He says something to the barman and then walks me to the

lift. My heart is racing. I don't know what to expect. We step inside the lift ... The doors close ... He slams me back against the mirrored wall ... He grabs hold of both hands and holds them above my head ... "Don't move ... don't make a sound ..."

Is he for real? I feel the heat between my legs and I want to squirm and wriggle. "Whiskey ..."

OK, I won't move then.

He leans forward and puts his spare hand on my thigh, just where the split in my dress is. He groans as his hand touches my skin, the spark of electricity igniting his thirst for me. He kisses me and at the same time his hand is moving extremely slowly up my thigh, towards ... towards ...

The lift pings and he pulls himself away from me and stands behind me as someone gets into the lift. I can feel his hardened cock against my thigh. It feels huge. I feel the heat pool between my legs and I let out a small moan.

He growls ... We are both breathing heavily. He moves forward slightly and kisses my neck just

under my ear and then he whispers "You're so lucky he stepped in here because I was just going to take you here in the lift. I was ready to press the alarm button and just fuck you. Do you feel what you've done to me?" He pushes closer and I can feel how much he wants me.

"Please ..." I whisper back. "Please what?"

"Please fuck me in the lift!" He moans, then the lift stops and the man gets out.

My heart is racing now. I know I asked him to fuck me in the lift, but I actually didn't think there would be an opportunity to. Now I'm scared, no not scared, I'm excited. When the lift door closes, he turns to face me. He has a grin on his face. "Hands above your head!" He orders. I comply.

Then he runs his finger all the way up my thigh

until it reaches my panties. He pulls them to one side and then he rips them off me. "Easier access." He states as he rolls them into a ball and puts them in his jacket pocket. His finger moves back and he runs it over my lips and my clitoris. "Oh my god, you're so wet!" He says licking his lips. "I want to taste you, but I'm going to wait. I want to be balls deep inside you right now and then I am going to take my time later on."

I groan, his finger feels so good flicking over my clitoris, he then thrusts his finger inside. "So tight!" he says as his other hand reaches inside his jacket and pulls out a condom. He reaches back and presses the alarm button on the lift and it comes to a shuddering stop.

"This won't take long," he says, as he takes his finger out and puts in a second one.

He puts the packet in his mouth and rips it so that he can take the condom out. He reaches down, opens his zip on his trousers and takes his cock out. He then puts the condom on with one hand. I'm impressed.

As soon as he has it on he takes his fingers out of me and replaces them with his cock. He lifts me so that I am straddling his waist and I move my hands to hold on.

"Brace yourself Whiskey. This is going to be hard!" He thrusts his cock inside me in one swift move.

I gasp, he fills me completely. I've never been so full before. It's a perfect fit.

He pushes deeper. "Fuck me hard Sawyer, please!" I can't wait any longer, I need this as much as he does. He starts thrusting, hard. It hurts ... no it doesn't hurt, it feels right.

He uses his finger to rub my clitoris and I can feel the orgasm building. I feel like I am on the verge of exploding and he only just entered me.

I move my hips as my back is resting against the mirror. I can see both of us on all four mirrored walls in the lift. It's strangely erotic, it's like watching a porn movie but being part of it and it turns me on even more.

"You like to watch yourself?" "Never done it before." "So much to do!" He says. He pushes deeper and

deeper, he rubs faster and faster. "Sawyer, I can't hold on." "Nearly there." He is pushing in and out really deep and it is hitting my spot. A voice comes into the lift. "Is everything ok in there?

You pressed the bell. Is the lift stuck?" "Fuck" he says. He shuffles me over so he can press the button to talk to the operator. "Of course it's stuck. Why do you think we pressed the alarm?" All the time he is talking he is pumping in and out and getting faster. I think it won't be long before he is going to explode. The operator better be gone soon, because I don't think I'll be able to keep quiet when I cum.

"Sir, we won't be long, I have an engineer on the way to fix it. Are you alone?"

Sawyer looks at me, smiling. "Don't say anything," he whispers.

He thrusts really hard and deep into me. "No, there is a woman here too. We're fine though, no panickers here."

"That's good, stay calm. We won't be long." The line disconnects.

Sawyer looks me in the eye, "He nearly put me off my stroke, but your pussy was clenching too tight for me to forget where I was."

He pushes ... I push ... "Sawyer, I really can't hold on any longer." I push

down one more time and then I explode around his cock. I've never come so hard before. I can see stars in front of my eyes.

He watches me unfold and can't hold any longer. "Fuck ... Whiskey ..."

He leans against me resting his forehead against mine after he has spilled all his cum inside me. He is breathing heavy. After a couple of minutes, he pulls his cock out of me and after taking the condom off he puts his cock back in his trousers. He slowly lets me down so that my feet are touching the ground. "Can you stand up?" He asks me as he can see I'm wobbly.

"I'll be fine, just give me a minute." He pulls me close to his body to support me.

"I just have to get the lift moving or we will be really embarrassed when the engineer turns up."

I forgot all about that. He leans past me and presses the button for his floor and the lift begins to move again. When it stops at his floor he takes my hand and pulls me out and down the corridor to his suite.

ABOUT THE AUTHOR

I hated English at school! Really hated it! I gave up on English Literature in fourth year because I hated writing stories; couldn't make them up to save my life.

I hated writing precis and I was horrendous at grammar.

Having lived in Norway when I was younger, English was my second language.

When I received my iPad six years ago I started reading on the kindle app and wrote to an author about how much I enjoyed her book.

That opened up the whole Facebook author world to me. I started reviewing books (ironic, right?) and then started beta reading (even more ironic) after pointing out some big mistakes in a book plot I was reviewing before release.

I realised I had a story in me, yeah I know everyone says that, but I really believed I did.

Thirteen books later ….

Welcome to the world of Krissy V!

For More Information:

www.krissyvauthor.com

MORE BOOKS FROM KRISSY V

Till Death Us Do Part Series

Till Death Us Do Part – The Trilogy in one book (Not available)

To Have and To Hold – Book 4 Standalone

For Richer or For Poorer – Book 5 Standalone

Sunshine Tours

Sunshine in Madrid

Sunshine at Christmas

Standalones

My One Regret

Beauty Within

0-Love in 6 Minutes

The Lust Train

A Taste of Christmas Dublin Style

Whiskey Sour

Whiskey

Snow

Mixology

Hunter

Keep your eyes on my facebook page:

www.facebook.com/authorkrissy.vas